Mistrust and Medicine in Mistletoe

Mistletoe Treasures

Book 2

By

Ronna M. Bacon

Verses

Lamentations 3:25 The Lord *is* good to those who wait for Him, To the soul *who* seeks Him.

Psalm 9:10 And those who know Your name will put their trust in You; For You, Lord, have not forsaken those who seek You.

Deuteronomy 4: **29** But from there you will seek the Lord your God, and you will find *Him* if you seek Him with all your heart and with all your soul.

New King James Version

Table of Contents

She crouched in her closet, praying he didn't find her that night. She hated him but was too young to leave home. Why, Lord, was her constant cry. She could hear him calling her and tried to make herself smaller. She knew when he found her, he would beat her and that she didn't want again. Her brother wasn't there to protect her. He said he was coming back for her, but he hadn't come. She hadn't seen him in three years and missed him.

The closet door was yanked open and the clothing roughly shoved aside as her arm was grabbed and she was hauled from her hiding spot. She saw the murder in his eyes and knew tonight, it just might happen. She could hear her mother talking, but she wasn't trying to help her. She was talking about how bad she was, how ungrateful, that she should be sharing her fortune with them. The girl, teen, young woman, for she was in her early twenties by now, didn't know what she meant.

Twenty minutes later, she lay in a broken heap, her back bruised and battered, blood seeping from numerous cuts. She lay there, unable or unwilling to move, knowing if she did, he'd only return. She missed her real daddy, she thought. Why, God, did you take him and bring this monster into my life?

She finally crept to her bathroom and into the shower, tears falling as the water from the shower stung and then soothed. She couldn't dress her wounds, not where they were. She slipped into her night clothes and then into her bed, her eyes red but dry, her tears all fallen. She stared at the window, praying for death, praying for relief, but knowing she'd have to rise early the next morning, put on her dress clothes and go to the job she hated but one that she had no choice about. He had almost broken her that night. It was only a matter of time, she thought. Lord, I don't know why, but I'm in Your hands. Protect me. Help me to find somewhere I can run to. Help me to get away from this monster they want me to call father, but that I can't. You know I can't do that.

She shuddered at the thought, her eyes finally closing as she slept. She didn't see the dark form move away from the house, anger burning inside him. He had heard her cries and pleas to stop but knew the police wouldn't interfere. He needed to find her help and soon. His eyes raised to the sky as he prayed as he had never prayed before. Please, dear Lord, protect this child of Yours.

Chapter 1

Levi Blackwell, or Blackie as he was known to his friends, studied the form in front of him and finally tossed it aside, running his hands through his golden blond curls. He wasn't interested in becoming a paramedic, he knew that for sure, but just what he wanted to do, that was the question. The town doctor has asked, no, he thought, had begged him to stay and become a paramedic for the town. That was something he knew he just couldn't do. He had had too many nights of awakening, drench in sweat, at the dreams he experienced after his eight years in the armed forces. He knew he just couldn't do that any more. Right now, he was seated at a desk in the small town of Mistletoe, brought there by a letter from a lawyer, a lawyer for his friend, Jacob Whitson. Only the lawyer had been arrested for the murder of his friend's grandfather and was behind the adventure his friend and his lady had drawn him into.

He raised his head as he heard voices from the reception area, one he recognized as Jacob's. The other, a female voice, he didn't know. He scooted his chair back enough he could see out the door, but could only see Jacob. He could hear Jacob's laughter as he teased whoever it was out there and her quiet response and laughter.

He listened as he heard Jacob thanking her for the food she had brought and then his laughter at her comment that Josh told her she had to hand deliver the order to Blackie. Jacob told her he was in the back office and to head that way, but before she could reply, her phone rang.

Then, a sharp exclamation came in her voice, and he was on his feet, heading that way, catching the grim look on Jacob's face. He watched as the woman turned back to face Jacob, concern etched on her face as she spoke into her phone.

"Give me ten minutes to change and I'll meet you at the entrance to the trail. The only thing is, we don't have a medic to go with us. Paul's out of town this week." She pocketed her phone, turning towards the door, as Jacob's hand came out to stop her.

"Julia? What's the problem?"

She spun, her long dark brown hair sparking with red highlights as her hazel eyes turned to him. "The Evans' youngest girl is missing. She's six. We're heading out to search for her. I guess from what Donald said, she's been missing since earlier this morning and no one realized it."

"Do you need help on the search and rescue?"

She nodded. "We can use the help. But what we need is someone with medical training."

"The concern being?" Jacob's eyes met Blackie's amber ones, a question in them.

"She's deaf, Jacob. She's not going to hear us calling her. Donald will have his dog, but we need someone who can assess her when we find her. The weather's to change this afternoon for the worse."

"Blackie? Can you help?" Jacob turned back to his friend, a plea in his eyes that Julia couldn't see.

Blackie started to shake his head, then caught the look of fear on Julia's face. He shrugged. "What all you do need?"

Julia spun at the new voice, startled, a hand going to her throat. "Excuse me?"

"I asked what you needed." Blackie sighed. As much as he hated to admit it to himself, he couldn't walk away from anyone in need, particularly a young child. "I was a medic in the armed forces."

Julia's face lit up. "You were? Do you have some time that you can use to help us search? I can't guarantee how long it will take."

Blackie shook his head. "That's not important. It's important that we find this young girl. I need to swing by the B&B and grab some gear. Where are we meeting?"

She frowned before looking at Jacob, who grinned at her.

"This is my friend, Levi Blackwell, or Blackie as we call him. Blackie, this is Julia Whittaker."

She nodded at him, then tilted her head. "Are you sure?"

He nodded. "Just let me know where to meet you and I'll be there."

Thirty minutes later, Blackie stood watching at the search and rescue team sorted itself out. He studied the ground, a frown in place, not seeing the small footprints in the bits of snow that he would expect. He raised his eyes to the sky, seeing the gray clouds, and knew that with only two weeks to Christmas, they would likely have snow today.

Julia approached him. "You're with me. Have you done search and rescue before?"

He gave an abrupt nod. "In the armed forces."

She paused, a look crossing her face he couldn't read, before she pointed to one of the trails. "We're taking that one."

"I don't see any small footprints." Blackie looked around once more.

"I know. That's bizarre. I would think there would be. But her father insists she came out here. I don't know the reasoning. We have to check this out, then move on."

Blackie nodded as he shouldered his pack, tugged his knitted hat down lower on his ears and forehead and pulled on his gloves. "I'll follow You know the area."

They didn't see the man standing back in the shadows, watching the search teams move out, or see him head after them. He had been hired to get Julia in any way he could. Having a man with her complicated things.

Snow began falling about an hour after they set out. Blackie finally pulled Julia to a stop.

"We'll never find her in this."

She nodded, fear on her face. "I know. And because she can't hear us, that makes it worse." She turned as she heard a noise, heading towards it.

Blackie's hand reached out. "Let me go first, please?"

She shook her heard. "You're not trained in this type of search and rescue. I am." She pulled away, even as she heard the roar of an ATV approaching.

Blackie spun, then dove for Julia, wrapping his arms around her and throwing them both away from the trail. A glancing blow from the machine sent them off balance and tumbling over the edge of a ridge, to roll and slide down to the bottom. The man on the ATV stood, trying to spot them through the snow and unable to. He finally left, hoping that what he had been hired to accomplish had been done. If not, he'd have to try again.

Chapter 2

Looking around as he heard his name called, Jacob waited for his friends, Simon and Josh, to catch up with him. He didn't like the looks on their faces.

"Whit, have you seen Blackie since this morning?" Simon Gardner was an officer with the county police.

Jacob shook his head, a small grimace crossing his face. "He headed out with Julia on that search and rescue."

"What search and rescue?" Simon studied the area around them, always on alert.

"Something about the youngest Evans girl? She spoke with Donald and then Blackie volunteered as they needed someone with medical training."

"I don't like that." Simon pointed back at the office building Jacob had just locked up. "Can we go inside out of the snow?"

Stamping their boots as they entered, Jacob motioned to the chairs in the reception area. "We can sit there or head for my office."

"Your office, I think, Whit. We may need the computer and your phone." Simon headed that way. "What time did they head out?"

"Around 10, maybe? It was just after you sent Julia here with the food, Josh." He looked over at his friend, sitting at his computer, and booting it up.

"That would be about right. It's now 4? And you haven't seen them since?" Josh shared a look with Simon.

"We received word this morning that a hoax was being played out here in Mistletoe, Jacob. We've just been able to sort it out. Someone is after Julia and staged the disappearance of the Evans' girl."

Jacob stilled, his hand resting on the coffee pot he had reached to fill. "There was no disappearance? They're out in this weather for nothing?" At their nod, he replaced the coffee pot and reached for his jacket and gloves. "We need to go find Donald and see what he has to say."

Josh started at the computer. "I'm going to stay and see what research I can do for you, Simon. I may need to call Blackie's father and I don't want to do that until we know for sure what's going on."

Simon shook his head. "No, not a good idea. I'll call as soon as we find out anything at all. You have the names of those on the search team?"

Josh looked up, his eyes meeting Jacob, and then quickly scrawling them done, handing it to Simon. "I do, Simon. I've gotten to know them over the last year and I can't see one of them being involved." He sighed. "But then Jacob didn't see it coming with his lawyer, so who knows the name of the culprit this time."

Simon agreed. "Before we move off, let's spend some time in prayer. We need God's guidance on this one, I'm thinking."

❄ ❄ ❄ ❄ ❄ ❄

Raising his head slightly, Blackie tried to move, finding himself unable to do so.

He groaned as he stirred, his eyes blinking open to snow, the flakes large and soft as they tickled down on his face. He blinked again, trying to orient himself and unable to do so. He could feel his pack digging into his back and sharp pain in his left shoulder. He tried to reach for it and couldn't, for a moment unsure why. Then, becoming more alert, despite the cold and the pain, he looked around him and realized he had a lady wrapped tight in his arms. He frowned through the pain, not remembering who she was or even where they were. He finally raised himself up enough to move away from her, laying her gently down, before he stood, staggering a bit before he caught his balance.

Lord, where am I? I don't remember where I am. I think I know my name, but even that is a blur. He turned, pain driving him to his knees as he clutched his arm to himself. He groaned once more, knowing he had to move, had to get them both to safety, but knowing he was unable to. He tried to reach his phone and realized he didn't have it with him. Where was it, he thought?

He turned to his pack, pulling out a scarf to fashion a makeshift sling, and then reaching back in for some thermal aluminum blankets he had stuck in at the last moment. Moving very slowly and cautiously he scraped snow away from the shelter of the rocks and draped the first blanket down the rocks themselves and across the ground as much as he could. He stood, head bowed, as he gathered breath and strength to move once more.

Shifting the packs to make a windbreak, he crept on his knees towards the lady, stopping once more to study her. He shook his head, pain wracking through him at that. He didn't know her, did he? As carefully as he could, he gathered her close and crept slowly back to the shelter he had erected, sitting with his back to the rocks, cradling her close to keep her warm and drawing the remaining two blankets over them, tucking them in as best he could.

I've done what I can, Lord. Lead someone to us. I can't get us out of here, and this lady can't help either. He tilted his head for a moment to stare down at her before his eyes slid closed.

Simon looked around at the trail, watching as Donald searched for tracks.

"They did come this way, Donald?"

Donald, a local contractor, looked up at Simon's words, his eyes catching his, before he looked past him at Josh and Jacob. "They did. Julia started off on this trail." He looked around again. "With the snow, it's hard to catch their tracks. I have Betty bringing in her dog to help track them." He glanced up at the sky. "It's clearing and that means the temperature will drop."

"In other words, we need find them and now, before night totally falls." Simon paced the area, his eyes searching the ground, a frown on his face. He shared looks with Josh and Jacob, who nodded and then moved to each side of the trail, both searching even as Simon moved back to the middle of the trail, Donald watching them before he shook his head and moved away. His thoughts were that they had no clue what they were doing and they would just destroy the scent trail.

Simon looked up as he heard Josh call quietly to him from where he stood near the edge of the trial.

"What did you find, Josh?" Simon stood, his eyes on his friend before he looked over the edge of the ridge, a frown in place.

"Someone went over the edge, I think, Simon. I'm afraid it was Blackie." Josh looked around. "It's not that far down. I see a spot further along where we can get down to that area."

"Lead the way." Simon turned to find Jacob standing with them, ready to head over the edge as well.

They had disappeared by the time Donald had returned with Betty. He was angry, and Betty could get no reason for it from him. Her dog headed for the same area where the three men had stood.

"They were here, Donald, and for some reason have disappeared."

"They can't just have disappeared, Betty. You know that."

"What I know is that I think you've been leading us on a wild goose chase and

21

caused harm to someone." She spoke to her dog and followed the men's footsteps, finding the trail they had taken.

Simon stood for a moment, his eyes searching the area before he felt Jacob's hand on his arm. He turned to where Jacob pointed, even as he heard Josh give a cry and drop to his knees there, pulling out the backpacks Blackie had stacked against the wind.

"Simon! Jacob!" He turned, his arm waving at them. "I've found them. Pray they're still alive."

The two other men scrambled through the snow, their feet slipping as they rushed forward. They could hear a woman's voice behind them, calling for them to wait.

Josh had dropped to his knees besides the two, carefully pulling back the blankets.

"Josh?" Simon was on the other side of them, bending over even as Jacob reached for the blankets.

"They're alive, Simon. I don't know how but they are. It looks as if Blackie's hurt in some way. I can't tell about Julia, though. Help me move them."

Hands reached for both Blackie and Julia. Blackie's arm tightened on Julia, refusing to give her up. Simon shook his head before he leaned over to Blackie and spoke.

"Blackie, it's us. Come on, now. Let us have the lady. We'll take care of her for you."

Blackie roused slightly, his eyes flickering open and closed, before he sank back into blackness. Jacob reached for Julia, turning to lay her on one of the blankets even as Betty dropped beside him.

"She's alive?"

"She is, Betty. How, I don't know. Blackie seemed to do what he could to keep them both that way." Jacob looked around, his eyes on his three friends, then back on Betty. "Can you have the ambulance meet us at the beginning of the trail? We're not that far away."

"No, we're not. They can have the stretchers up top." She stood, her hand shading her eyes against the setting sun as she searched for Donald. "Now, where did he get to?"

"Who? Donald? Didn't he wait?"

She shook her head. "Doesn't look like it. Something's been off with this whole thing, Jacob. We'll need to look into it." She turned. "I'll head up where I can get some cell service and make the call. Can you three manage to get them up top?"

"We can. Go." Jacob watched as Betty ran as fast as she could through the snow, her dog on her heels.

"Jacob? How's Julia?"

"Not as cold as I thought. But she has a nasty cut on her head." Jacob turned to watch Blackie. "How's Blackie?"

"Dislocated shoulder, I think. And he seems to have taken the brunt of the cold." Josh stood for a moment. "Where's Donald? I thought he'd be here."

"That's what Betty asked. She's heading up to call for help. Can we manage to get them up there?"

"It will be easy for Julia. With Blackie, no matter how we carry him, it will hurt."

"He's not up to walking out, that's for sure." Simon stood for a moment. "I've swing him over my shoulders and carry him out. Can you to manage the packs?"

"We can. Let's get them out of here."

The three friends stood watching as the paramedics worked on the couple before Simon walked towards the ambulance, climbing aboard and finding a seat. He nodded at his friends as the doors shut and the vehicle moved off, gathering speed as it hit clearer roads.

Betty spoke from beside Jacob. "How are they?"

Jacob shrugged. "They didn't really know. Blackie's shoulder is hurt, that's about all." He locked around. "Where's Donald?"

Betty shook her head. "I have no idea. I haven't seen him."

Josh nodded. "Find him. I want to talk with him. So will Simon, not just as a friend of Blackie's, but as law enforcement. Something tells me this was all a set up." He turned and walked away with Jacob, leaving Betty staring at them, her mouth open before she snapped it shut and silently agreed with them. This was a set up, she thought. But which one was it? Julia who had lived her all her life? Or Blackie, new to town but a descendant of the founding families?

Chapter 3

Shaking his head in disbelief, Blackie shifted on the bed. grimacing slightly at the pain from his shoulder, dislocated in the fall but now repaired.

"There is no way I'd be out in a snow storm, guys. You know me better than that." He glared at Josh and Jacob as they laughed at him.

"You were, trust us on that, Blackie. You volunteered to help search for a young girl." Jacob stopped, his eyes on the doorway where Simon stood. "Only thing is, we can't figure out how you two ended up where you did."

"Two? There were two of us?"

Josh nodded, a grin on his face. "There were two. You headed out with Julia, then never came back. We went looking for you and found you."

Blackie shook his head again, sitting up to the side of the bed and reaching for the bag of clothes Josh had set on it. "I still don't see me doing that. You know me and search and rescues now."

"We do, but you went anyway." Jacob's hand steadied him as he stood, heading for the bathroom to change.

"How'd we end up where we did?" His voice came through the door.

"That's what we're working on, Blackie. From what the physician said, it looks as if you were struck a glancing blow to the side, likely from an ATV, and sent over the side of the ridge. Until we find the driver or either of you remember what happened, we won't know for sure."

The door popped open and Blackie stood there, sling in hand. "Doesn't this Julia remember?" He allowed Jacob to adjust the sling for him.

Simon shook his head. "I haven't had a chance to talk with her. She was unconscious when you came in last night. I'm heading that way now."

"Not without me, you're not." Blackie reached for his jacket and wallet. "I don't have my phone with me."

Jacob stared at him. "You don't? You never go anywhere without it."

"I know. That's what's so strange." He walked towards the door, as Simon's hand came out to stop him.

"Blackie, we need to pray over this. Someone likely tried to kill one of you yesterday. I don't know which one. I've talked to the force here. They can't figure it out, but there's something they are not saying about Julia, and I have no idea what it is."

Blackie stood for a moment in the hospital room door, watching the young woman who stood near the bed, folding her hospital gown, before she looked up. He winced as he saw how white she was, the dark circles under her eyes.

Julia had sensed someone watching her and glanced up, her gaze locking with Blackie's. Her eyes searched his face for a moment before she gave an inward sigh. Not someone else to walk in and walk out of my life. Lord, I need someone to protect me. I know You do, but it would be nice to have someone here, to stand between me and the harassment and brutalities I face.

"Hi." Blackie walked towards her, stopping abruptly when he saw fear flicker across her face and a slight withdrawing. "You must be Julia. I'm sorry I don't remember us meeting before today, but I sure wish I did."

Julia frowned, her head tilted as she watched his face and saw the honesty and something else she couldn't read on it. "That's right. I'm Julia. You were kind enough to help search yesterday." She sighed. "Only I hear tell we didn't get too far."

"Do you remember what happened?"

"I do, unfortunately. I saw something off the trail, went to look at it, heard you yell, and then we were falling. I remember an ATV there." She looked up, fear in her eyes. "Who was it, Blackie? May I call you that?" At his nod, she continued. "Who did that? They left us for dead, you know."

"I know. I have no idea. Simon is working on that with the Mistletoe force." He looked at the door and then back at her. "Do you have a ride somewhere?"

She shook her head, even as the door slammed back against the wall and a tall hulking man entered. She gave a stifled scream and moved back, her face full of fear.

Blackie watched the man, ready to step in if needed.

"You just had to go and do that, didn't you?" The man stood, fists clenched, staring down at Julia.

"Do what?"

"Be found like you were. Always chasing after some guy, aren't you?" The man's hand raised and struck Julia across the face, knocking her into the bed.

Blackie gave a cry of rage and jumped towards the man, his right hand catching his arm and spinning him around. No match for him with only one arm, Blackie tumbled backwards as the man's fist connected with his jaw, slamming into the door frame and then crumpling to the floor, to lie in a still heap.

The man turned back to Julia, curses raining down on her as his hand came back to once more strike her, this time drawing blood from her mouth.

Simon slid to a stop in the doorway, instantly assessing the situation and together with Jacob, approaching the man and taking him to the floor, holding him there despite his struggles. A lucky blow from the man's hand caught Simon's across the eyes, temporarily blinding him as he felt for his hand cuffs. He blinked rapidly and snapped the cuffs in place, hauling the man to his feet and to the door. Tom, one of the town officers, stood there, ready to take control on Simon's prisoner.

"I would be quiet, man, if I were you." Tom read the man his rights, finally getting through to him that he was under arrest.

The man struggled to turn, his eyes seeking Julia, hatred and murder in them, before Tom hauled him away.

Jacob was on his knees beside Blackie, even as Blackie righted himself and leaned back agains the wall. Blackie's eyes sought Julia, wincing at the red hand print on her face and the blood on her mouth.

"Help me up, Jacob." Jacob helped Blackie, despite protesting such a move.

Blackie moved towards Julia, stopping as she cringed back from him.

"Julia? We need to get your face looked at."

She shrugged. "Why? They won't do anything. They never had before, so why now?"

"This isn't the first time?" Simon stood beside Blackie, a dark look on his face. "The police did nothing?"

She shook her head. "Why would they? He's Chief Adams brother-in-law. Unfortunately, he's married to my mother." She held up a hand at their protest. "No, he's not my father. Thank God for that." She looked past him at the older physician and sighed. "All right, Paul. You can look and take pictures, but it won't do any good."

"It will this time, Julia. Adams is out of being in control as are a lot of his cronies. Simon here is helping out to restructure our force. He'll listen." Paul, the physician, shot a look at Simon's face. "And it looks as if Hal has assault on an officer added to the charges today."

"He's done that before and it's always been shuffled under the rug." She stood, gathering the bag she had been given. "Why does God let this happen, Paul? We've discussed this before. No one can tell me that."

Paul nodded towards Blackie. "Ask him. He's not from this town. He may have an answer for you we don't."

Her gaze shifted to Blackie, catching that expression on his face again and she frowned even as Paul set her down on the bed and assessed her face. She winced as he touched the mark.

"It's going to bruise, Julia. How many times has this happened to you?"

She shrugged, her eyes still on Blackie. "Too many, I guess. But you know. I've tried to report it and been told it's my fault." The men heard the pleading and the tears in her voice even as she blinked rapidly. "No one, except you, has ever believed me. Jonathan took off as soon as he could, and that was fifteen years ago, when he was 17, to escape this. And Hal usually didn't hit where it showed."

"I know, Julia. That still doesn't make it acceptable or right." He looked up at the men standing there, catching the look on Blackie's face, and nodded. Good, he thought. God has finally brought in a rescuer for Julia. It's about time. Thank you, Lord. Protect them both. Hal won't take the arrest quietly.

Julia finally stood, reaching for her bag, to find Josh had already picked it up, grinning at her as she frowned. Jacob and Simon had already headed out for the vehicle, Josh following them. Blackie hesitated for a moment.

"Where do you want to go, Julia?"

She shrugged. "I can't go to Mom's. She's always stuck up for him and having had him arrested, she'll be as livid with me as he was." She sighed. "I have no idea, Blackie. It doesn't look as if I'm wanted in this town."

Blackie wrapped an arm around her, feeling her stiffen and then relax against him as he walked her towards the door. "Finn's parents have a room available, I know. Or they did. If they don't, you can have mine and I'll bunk in with Jacob. That won't be the first time we've done that."

She shook her head. "They won't do that."

Blackie grinned, even as he tucked her into Jacob's truck and slid in beside her. "They will. I'm sure you know Finn."

"Everyone in town knows Finn. And yes, I do. We had classes together." She stared out the window. "I need to stop by Mom's and collect some clothes. I'll also need to pack up my stuff on another day and find somewhere else to live. I can't go back there."

"We'll take you today, Jewel, and then back again on whatever day you want. And we'll find you somewhere you can live. Between the four of us here and Finn's family, we own quite a few buildings in town." Blackie shared a look with Simon and then Jacob. Josh had headed back to his cafe to make sure all was set for Monday

She spun, surprise on her face. "How is that possible?   None of you are from town? Other than Finn."

"We're all descendants, believe it or not, of the town's founders.   We've been brought back here for a purpose, what purpose we're still working on."   Blackie watched the emotions flicker across her face, hope rising within her.

Chapter 4

*B*lackie stood just inside the house door, listening to the abuse and berating that Julia was facing from her mother. His heart broke, knowing he would never hear those words from his own mother, and wishing desperately he could just pack Julia up and take her to his home. He knew his mother would just sweep her into her arms and give her the biggest hug as would his father. His two sisters would just take her over and make her part of the family.

He looked up as he heard her footsteps coming towards him, rapid, almost running. He caught her into a one-armed hug and pulled her out of the house, the abuse continuing as he tucked her back into the truck. He stood for a moment, staring back at the open door and then shaking his head, a prayer raised for protection and healing for his Jewel, he crawled in beside her, reaching to cradle her against him, sharing a long look with Simon, who nodded and then pulled away from the curb.

She turned her face into Blackie's shoulder, surprised that she didn't fear him, in fact, welcomed his arm around her. She felt cherished, something she hadn't since her own father had died when she was five. She finally raised her head, to find Simon pulling up in front of Finn's parents' B&B. She hesitated as Blackie slid out and reached for her hand, not letting go as he walked her up and into the house and then back into the private living quarters, despite her protest that she didn't belong there.

Finn's mother, Mary Bronagh, looked up, a smile of greeting on her face. Her hands were deep in pastry as she prepared desserts for her guests.

Jacob walked around the counter and dropped a kiss on her cheek. He was family as far as they were concerned, now dating their daughter, Finn.

"Blackie, who do you have here?" Mary's face was alight with her smile, no censure seen at all.

"This is Julia Whittaker. I'm not sure if you have ever met."

Mary brushed the pastry from her hands and then washed them, dropping the towel she had dried them with on the counter.

"I have. At church. I have so wanted to get to know you better, Julia, but you have been gone before I can find you. Welcome to our home. Please have a seat. These boys just take it for granted they can help themselves to food and coffee or tea. Which would you prefer? Or I have hot chocolate and hot cider on the stove."

Julia hesitated as Mary stood, her hands on her arms after having hugged her. She had never had a greeting like this before.

"Oh, whatever is easiest, I guess."

Mary directed her to a chair. "Now, that's not how it works in this house. Which do you prefer? That's how it works. And I have some Christmas baking here, if the boys haven't eaten it all."

Blackie slid into a chair beside Julia. "Not yet, we haven't." He reached for a cookie from the plate he had set down and then shoved the plate towards Julia. "Here, Jewel. You need something. Hospital food is not fit to eat."

Julia gave a surprised laugh, her look questioning as she once again caught the name he was using for her. He stared at her, then winked, causing her to blush.

Josh handed Blackie his phone. "Mary found this on the table in the hall yesterday. She said your dad called here looking for you."

Blackie nodded, as he slipped the phone into his pocket. "I'll call him later. He'll understand."

Julia stared at him. "He'll understand? Just like that? You don't have to call him and apologize over and over for not calling him sooner?"

Blackie blinked at the vehemence in her voice before he shook his head. "No, I don't have to. Dad knows I'll call when I can. He understands. He always has. And with me having been in the armed forces, he knows there are times he'll call and I can't answer for a day or so."

Julia's hand dropped from the mug she had been reaching for. "You were in the armed forces? What did you do there?"

Blackie sighed, not wanting to say it out loud but knowing he had no choice. "I was a medic. And no, I'm not going to become a paramedic just because this town has need of one. That's not where God is calling me. And I have to follow that calling, not my own."

She shook her head, not quite believing what she was hearing. The four in the kitchen with her exchanged looks before Blackie reached for her hand. She started, then stared at his hand gripping hers before she raised her eyes.

"My family understands what it's like for me to be away from home and unable to call them. Even my two sisters are allowed a certain amount of leeway but they know when to call our parents and when not to. Mom and Dad have drilled it into our heads. They allow us the freedom to come and go." He paused, biting at his lip, not quite sure how to proceed.

"I never ever had that, Blackie." Her voice was so low, he could barely catch her words. "I had to report at designated times. I wasn't allowed to move around freely. If I did, I paid for it." She raised her eyes to Mary, finding compassion and understanding there. "I need to break away from them but I don't know how. I have never had anyone who would stand up for me. If I tried to leave, I got dragged back. Even as an adult, my life was controlled." She brushed at the tears rolling down her face. "Hal or his buddies made sure of that. They seemed to think they owned a portion of the town, but I know better." She looked at Simon. "Simon, I have documents hidden away that I need to give you, You'll need them. Hal and his buddies are involved in something here in town, but I'm not sure what. I hope you can find out."

Simon nodded, even as he lifted his mug to have a drink. "Just let me have them when you get them. The important thing now is that you're out of that house. Mary, can she stay here for at least tonight? Until we can make other arrangements for her?"

"She can stay here as long as she likes. You know how we're set up. There's the empty room beside Finn's that she can have, with the shared bath and door opening to both rooms. Finn will love that. She always wanted a sister, but God didn't choose to let us have any more than the two."

Blackie reached for Julia's hand, clasping hers in his, his eyes on her face, his heart raised in prayer. Lord, there's something special about this lady, and I'm not sure where I'm headed but I know I'm in for an adventure, at the very least. Protect her please. Help her to find the treasure she's seeking and doesn't know she is and doesn't know how to find.

Julia's eyes searched the faces watching her and didn't find what she expected. She didn't find dislike, hatred, censure. Instead, she found compassion, love, warmth, and something else she just couldn't put into words. She felt welcome. Tears gathered in her eyes and her head went down on her hands. Mary rose and came around the table, her arms around the young woman, even as she heard movement from the men as they stood and walked from the room, to let Mary have time with the young woman, time to show her what a mother's heart was like.

Finn stood for a moment in the doorway, watching her mother. She frowned, then her face cleared. Julia! Wonderful, she thought. I want to know this lady better. We've had contact, Lord, but not enough. Help us to help her

Mary looked up as she heard footsteps, and greeted her daughter. "We have a guest for a while, love. Julia has come to stay. Is the room next to yours ready for our friend?"

"It always is, Mom. I'm so glad she's here." Finn had questions that she would ask later. "Hi, Julia. Let's get you upstairs and settled before supper. I can smell the chicken potpie Mom has in the oven. It will be ready soon."

Mary nodded as Finn linked her arm with Julia's and led her up the back stairs.

Julia stood for a moment in the doorway of the room, taking in the canopy bed, the oak furnishings, the warm peach and cream colourings, and shook her head. "This is too nice for me, Finn. I can't stay here."

"You can and you will. See, Mom has already designated this as Julia's room. Please?" Finn knew she was begging and wasn't about using her mother as a bargaining chip. "It looks as if the guys had put your belongings in here. That door there, it leads to my room. It's unlocked and open to you at any time of the day or night. Come find me if you need me." Finn led her to the other door. "This is your bathroom. I hope it's okay." She watched in compassion as tears rolled down Julia's face.

"I have never had anything so nice. You wouldn't want to see the room I have been living in, or the shabby, broken down bathroom I've had to use."

"No more. Not if Blackie has anything to say about it."

Julia spun to stare at her. "Blackie? Why would he care?"

"Because he cares what happens to you. I can see he cares for you. He wouldn't have brought you here if he hadn't." Finn pointed to the bathroom. "Go on. You've time for a shower if you want. I'll lend you some of my clothes for tonight if you like." Finn almost danced across the

46

room. "This is going to be so much fun. I always wanted a sister to share things with and now I have one." She disappeared through the door into her room.

Julia stared, open mouthed, after her before her jaw clamped closed and she shook her head. She stepped into the bathroom, awed by the colours and the design and the cleanliness of it. No matter how she tried, she couldn't get her bathroom this clean. It was just impossible.

Finn searched her clothing, finding just the right peach sweater and grey cords for Julia. She knew her mother would agree that Julia needed some new clothes. Her clothes were neat, but worn and faded.

Blackie turned to face Simon as he paced the office. They were alone for the moment, Jacob and Josh heading out to shovel snow.

"Simon? What is going on with Julia?"

Simon shrugged. "I have no idea, Blackie, but something is. We've been watching her stepfather for a while now, from what I can tell. He's involved in something here in town. Maybe that's why you've been brought to town. You're likely the one who can get through to Julia. She's responding to you like she doesn't with anyone else. Just like Finn did with Jacob."

Blackie stopped his pacing, turning once more to Simon. "There's something about her. She looks fragile but she has an inner strength in there." He sighed. "I heard that her boss fired her, likely on the instructions of Hal. We need to find her something to do."

Simon nodded. "Her boss is a crony of Hal's. That's how he controlled her."

Blackie nodded. "We have to watch her. He'll try and take her again. He's not the type to let her just walk away. It's a matter of life and death with her."

"That it is, Blackie." Simon turned as Jacob and Timothy, Finn's father, entered the office.

Timothy spoke. "I heard what you said, and you are correct, Simon. We have tried for years to get her away from him and never succeeded. Not until Blackie here."

He paused, lost in thought. "But Blackie's right, we need to find her something to do."

Jacob spoke up. "I could employ her. My business is growing to the point I need a secretary. If that's what she has been going, I'll gladly offer her work."

Blackie turned to his friend, before nodding. "That would work. With both of us in the office, that would help to keep her safe. But we need to find out what it is she has hidden away and how it affects this town. I just know it does."

His friends laughed at his tone of voice, knowing he would be investigating until he found the answer.

Chapter 5

$\mathcal{J}$ulia turned in a circle, studying the reception area of Jacob's business office, before nodding. She looked up to find Blackie watching her, a small smile on his face.

"Do you think you could work here?"

She sighed. "I suppose. It's too nice, though. I'm not used to this."

"It's not as nice as some offices I've seen. Jacob has only set up the bare bones of it. We'll need your help to expand what he started." He pointed to the counter. "That's there for your protection. No one comes past it without an appointment with either Jacob or myself. Make sure you follow that directive, please?"

She once more nodded, fear flickering across her face. She came around the counter and stood staring at her work station. "I've never had such a nice work area. I don't think I'll get anything done."

Blackie linked his arm with hers. He had discarded the sling, much to her protest. He turned her towards the rest of the office.

"Now, Jacob's office is right behind yours. He's there most days. Sometimes he'll have to travel, but on those days, if I can't be here, you're not here. The office will be closed. Understood?" He waited for her nod. "Now, this is my office, right across from Jacob's. I can see your work station if I move back from the desk and I will if I hear anything I don't like. I don't have to travel. Not yet anyway. My investigations are done on the internet and I communicate back and forth with my father. I work for him but can work from anywhere. Back here is the lunch room. It has a secondary exit to the back of the building. We've also put in a strong door and lock. If you're concerned or scared, head here and lock the door. There is a cell phone kept here at all times. It has all our numbers programmed into it for you."

Julia stood for a moment, staring around the room, before looking at Blackie.

"Why?"

"Why what?"

"Why go to all this for me?"

"Because you're worth it, Julia. Whether you believe it yet or not, you are definitely worth it. Now, about your work. Let's head back to the desk and get you started. I don't have a lot right at the moment, but I know Jacob's work is taking off. You will be busy. And as for dress code. Don't dress up. You don't need to. Jeans are fine."

She spun to stare at him. "Jeans?" She managed to choke out the word.

"Jeans. We're not fancy and we don't expect many clients to come in. Jeans are just fine with both of us."

She was upset, he could tell. "I've never been able to dress like that for work, you know? Most of the little pittance I made had to go for fancy dress clothes, even though there were very few people through the office."

Blackie reached to hug her, waiting until she finally hugged him back before he spoke. "I know. Part of the control he wanted over you. That's in the past. I suspect he'll try and get to you again, but we'll do our best to protect you. And we need to find that paperwork you have to give Simon."

"It's at the house. I have it hidden there." She turned away from him, her shoulders slumping. "I just don't know how I'll ever get it or the rest of my belongings."

Blackie sighed, before reaching to place his hands on her shoulders. "We'll take Simon and Tom. As police officers, they will protect you and help you claim your belongings. Hal and your mother cannot get rid of anything of yours nor can they prevent you from taking it. Let me call Simon and set it up for tonight. He said Hal would be held in jail until at least tomorrow."

She turned, a troubled look on her face. "It's too much bother."

"No, it's not. Not for a friend. Not for someone who needs us. It's what we do, Jewel. It's who we are." Blackie watched as she thought that through, her head shaking.

"I've never had that, you know, not that I can remember. Jonathan tried before he left but Hal was so hard on him." Tears pooled in her eyes before she blinked them away. "I just wish I knew where he was."

"That, maybe, I can help you with. Let me have his full name and date of birth and I do some research."

She studied his face once more before she told him. "What time today, Blackie? Mom works until 5. If I can get in and out before then, I'd like that."

"Let me call Simon and see if we can go about three. How many boxes will you need?"

She gave him an incredulous look and a broken laugh before she ran for the rest room. She needed time to compose herself.

❄ ❄ ❄ ❄ ❄ ❄

Blackie reached for Julia's hand that afternoon as they sat at the curb outside her home, waiting for Simon and Tom

"I need to pray for you, Jewel." He reached for her hand.

She stared at him. "Really? You think God cares that much about us?"

"He does, Jewel. I know He does." Blackie closed his eyes as he prayed for their safety, wisdom in dealing with the situation, and for Julia, to know God's love for her.

She stared out the window, not responding when he was finished. He desperately wanted to reach her but didn't know how. He heard a vehicle and looked, watching as Simon and Tom each climbed from a cruiser.

"Are you ready, Jewel?"

She turned to eye him. "Not really, but let's get it over with. Mom will likely accuse me of theft, knowing her."

"That's why Simon and Tom are here. They will watch everything you pack, and verify that it is yours and that you're not taking anything that doesn't belong to you."

Simon reached for a couple of the boxes Blackie pulled from the back of his vehicle and nodded towards Julia. "How is she?"

"Broken. Hurting. Wanting this over with. I can't reach her, Simon."

"You have, Blackie." He walked towards the house, eyes watchful, and followed Julia into the house. "Where's your bedroom, Julia?"

"At the back of the house. That's all they'd allow me." Julia headed that way, not seeing the looks the three men shared.

Blackie noted the opulent look of the house and shook his head. It was not what he expected.

Simon spoke from behind him. "Tom will stay here by the door, just in case. You go help Julia. I'll be at the bedroom door. I have a bad feeling about this, Blackie."

"You and me both. Let's get her packed up and out of here. I'm sure the neighbours will have something to say."

Simon watched for a moment as Blackie headed for Julia before he followed.

Blackie stood watching Julia before he spoke.

"What can I do to help, Julia?"

She spun, surprise on her face before she shook her head. "I'm almost done, Blackie. I don't have a lot. Those two boxes can go. I have a duffle bag here with my clothes." She spun and almost ran for the closet. Blackie followed as she pulled at the trim on the inside of the closet door. She pulled on a packet of rolled paper and stuck it into the duffle bag. She looked around, sorrow on her face but also relief. "That's all, I think. If not, it can stay."

Blackie stopped her for a moment, his hand cupping her cheek. "You're sure?"

She nodded, then flinched as she heard a strident voice from the front of the house, chastising Tom, who stood in the doorway

"Is there a way we can get out back?"

She shook her head. "No. Hal made sure of that. I have to go back out through the front."

Blackie stopped her. "Stay behind Simon, as tight to him as you can. He'll take your boxes. Let me have your bag. I'll be right behind you. Don't stop and talk, just keep moving. Tom will keep your mother away from you, as will Simon."

She nodded, blinking rapidly before she moved towards Simon. Sandwiched between the two men, she walked away from the room that had been hers for so many years. She knew she would not be back, not unless something drastically changed.

Her mother stood on the porch, Tom standing in her way, as the three made their way from the house.

"Of course, you'd come when I wasn't home, wouldn't you? Hal said you would. I want to inspect those boxes and bags to make sure you're taking anything of mine." She reached past Tom, who caught her arm and stopped her. "What's the meaning of this?"

"The meaning of this is that Julia has taken only what is hers and hers only from her bedroom. She was watched by an officer of the law." Tom kept stepping in her way to stop her from moving towards Julia.

Blackie tucked her into his vehicle and slid behind the wheel, nodding at Simon as he waved them away before he headed back to the house.

Julia leaned her head back, drawing in a deep breath, flinching when Blackie's hand touched hers.

"Jewel?"

She finally nodded, raising her head and staring at Blackie. "Can I ask you something?" At his nod, she sighed. "You keep calling me Jewel. Why?"

"Why Jewel? Because that's how I see you, a precious jewel, an undiscovered treasure, something so precious and loveable that God sent His Son to die for you. I'm not sure where you stand on that, Jewel, but that's how I see you. You're important to me and I can't call you Julia when I think of you as that."

She shook her head. "This is all new, Blackie. I've never dated. Never been allowed to, even as an adult. Hal kept so tight a control I couldn't get away. His friends watched and tattled on me no matter what I did. I did try and escape a few times but paid the price in beatings."

Blackie drew a deep breath. "No more, not if I can help it, Jewel. Now, what about those papers you dug up? What's so important about them."

"I'm not sure. There are papers that Hal had as well as some limited research I did. It has something to do with land willed to descendants of the original founders. I have no idea who they are but maybe Simon can figure it out."

Blackie started to laugh, drawing a frown from her. He gave a small smirk before he spoke. "Seeing as I'm one of them as are Simon, Josh, Jacob and Finn, I'm sure we'll figure it out."

She gasped, a look of horror crossing her face. "You are? That must be what he meant."

"Who meant what?" Simon pulled into the B&B and turned off the ignition before turning to face Julia.

"Hal. He said something on the phone two weeks ago about needing to rid the town of the founders' descendants. Oh, Blackie, what have I done?"

"You done? Nothing. You didn't know. Now that we know, we can take precautions. Come on, let's get you inside."

Chapter 6

*S*imon looked up from the papers, thoughtful look on his face, before he turned to Julia.

"You really don't know what you have here, do you?"

She shook her head. "No, I'm sorry, Simon. I don't." She paced Timothy's study, her arms wrapped around herself. "I just grabbed a bunch of papers one day that Hal had left out. I'm not sure if he's even aware that he did that. It was about a year or so ago."

"That's about the time I was sent that letter and directed to the cafe." Josh leaned back in his chair, his eyes on Simon. "So, who really directed us all here?" He looked back over his shoulder at Jacob and Finn, who were researching on her father's computer.

"That's what I'd like to know. The lawyer Grand had, that Norman fellow, isn't talking. He has to know who it was." Jacob looked over at Blackie, who sat, his eyes on his laptop as he worked away. "Blackie?"

Blackie roused, his eyes raising to find them all staring at him. "What? Did I miss something?"

"You miss something whenever you don't hear what I say." Jacob smirked and ducked the crumpled ball of paper Blackie lobbed at him even as he laughed. "No, we were trying to figure out who set Norman up to get us all here."

Blackie nodded. "That's what I want to know, too. Someone gathered us all here for a reason." He rubbed his forehead, his eyes going back to his laptop and then he was lost to the rest of them as he delved back into his work

Josh shook his head. "What did you find out, Simon?"

Simon raised his head. "I'm still not sure, Josh.   There's something different about this that I need to study. There seems to be two or three different people involved in whatever it is Hal has become involved in."   His eyes focused on Julia and he frowned, catching Blackie's eyes once more as Blackie looked up. Simon shook his head at Blackie, who nodded.

Blackie's eyes focused on the email he was sending his father, telling him what was going on and attaching what he knew about Julia's brother and asking for him to search for Jonathan. He knew his father would search until he found something. A tone sounding on his laptop let him know that he had an email. His father had responded quickly, letting him know that he would search for the brother. Then a sentence at the end caught Blackie's eye, causing him to shoot a quick look at Julia, before he re-read it. "Have you found your princess?" his father asked. Blackie smiled, not quite sure if he had or not. Julia had issues that she needed to work through and finding freedom for the first time was one of them.

Simon finally packed the papers away into his briefcase. He needed to talk to his lieutenant and that would have to wait until tomorrow. First, he needed to get Blackie off on his own and find out what his thoughts were, and he knew that was going to be difficult, given how close he was staying to Julia.

Julia looked up as Finn dropped to the couch beside her and handed her a cup of hot chocolate. Finn studied her new friend, not quite sure how to ask what she wanted to. Julia finally sipped the chocolate, looking away from Finn. She wasn't quite comfortable with her, not knowing her. She sighed to herself, wished Blackie was there but he and Jacob were shut up in the office on a conference call of some kind and had been for at least an hour.

Finn finally spoke. "I have to go do shopping for presents. Do you want to come?"

Julia's head whipped around. "You're asking me to go shopping with you?"

Finn nodded. "I am. I know Mom wants to but she's busy right now trying to get all the baking done for the Christmas party for the kids at church."

"She's the one that does that?"

Finn stared at Julia. "You never knew?" When Julia shook her head, Finn reached for her hand and squeezed it. "Mom has done it for years. She just loves coming up with new designs and treats for the kids. We keep telling her to cut back but she always adds something new and takes away something."

Julia finally nodded. "I guess I can. I just don't know though. Blackie probably won't let me."

Finn looked behind Julia, catching the look on Blackie's face as he heard her words and then shifting her gaze to Jacob, who shook his head at her.

Julia jumped as she felt someone touch her arm and then shift her over enough so that he could sit beside her. She stared at Blackie for a moment, trying to read his face.

"I'll take you shopping with Finn, Julia. I won't stop you. You get to decide what you want to do and then we assess the risks and make it happen. You're not a prisoner." He nodded towards the door. "If you want, the door's always open. You can leave at any time you want. I just pray that you don't. We don't want to lose you, now that we've found you." Blackie met her eyes, finally reading her acceptance of his friendship there. She had always held something back, he felt.

"Okay, so when, Finn?" Her focus returned to the other woman, sitting with Jacob's arms tight around her, wishing it was that way with her, that Blackie's arms were around her. Now, where did that come from? Lord, I'm not too sure about You or about Blackie. I don't have a good father figure and that's what they say You are, a Father to us. You'll have to teach me, please, Lord.

"We'll make sure you stay safe, Julia." Jacob spoke up, his eyes on Blackie. "I suggest we go over to Merryville instead of shopping here. I've wanted to wander those shops." He laughed as Finn dug her elbow into his ribs. "You don't believe me?"

"No, I don't. I know how much you like shopping." She smirked at him before turning her attention back to Julia. "Tomorrow's Saturday. I have Anna working the shop and Peter said he'd help. Can we go tomorrow? We only have a couple of weeks left and I'm usually done my shopping by now."

Blackie nodded. "That works. Now, how be we head out to Josh's for dinner?"

Chapter 7

*C*ompassion filled Blackie the next day as he watched Julia wander through the shop, her fingers touching various objects and trinkets, but not buying anything. He realized she likely didn't have money to do any shopping. He approached, his hand on her arm.

"Julia, you can help me out here." She looked up, a question on her face. "I need to shop for my parents, my sisters, and then Finn's people. I have no idea what to get them."

She shrugged. "I have no idea either, Blackie. I was never allowed to shop. Mom always did that. She said I had no clue as to what to buy." She gave a harsh laugh. "It's hard to shop for people who hate you, especially when you have no money to do so." She blinked rapidly to clear her eyes.

Blackie looked around, feeling someone watching him but not seeing anyone that stood out. He gently drew Julia aside, his hand on hers as he stood for a moment watching her.

"Then, we'll shop together. I'd like to hear your ideas. Then the gifts can come from both of us."

Her gaze shot to his as she shook her head. "I can't do that."

"I can and I will." He grinned at her. "Now, my sisters are 20 and 16. What would they like? I was out of their lives for the eight years I was in the armed forces and am just getting to know them again."

She shook her head even as he dropped a kiss on her cheek, her eyes going towards the door before she sighed. "I just knew he'd have someone following me."

"Who? Hal? Where?"

"There by the door. That short man. He's a good friend of Hal's." She glared at him. "Now he'll go running to tell him you kissed me in a store."

Blackie laughed in an unrepentant manner as he hugged her. A couple with white hair and matching canes stopped, grins on their faces.

"I hope you two lovebirds have as long and happy a life as we have." The woman spoke, her eyes on the younger couple before she looked up at her husband. "Right, Frank?"

"That's right, Mae. Sixty five years that feel like we're just starting out. God bless you two young people."

Julia stared after them as they walked away. "But...". Her voice died away. "They think we're a couple."

"That's what I would like, Jewel." He watched the couple walk away, not catching the look on her face.

Blackie led her towards some scarves. "So, tell me. Would Rachel and Rebecca like these?"

She fingered them. "They're beautiful, Blackie. I'm sure they would. But what colours? They have such an amazing selection. And they're so soft." She held up a pale peach patterned one and Blackie knew somehow he had to sneak that into the pile for her.

"For Rachel, something soft. Blues, yellows, greens. Yes, that one. She'd like it.

For Rebecca, something gaudy." He laughed at her expression. "She's 16 and is in that gaudy phase." He watched as she sorted through the scarves, tucking the peach one into the pile he held before she saw him.

"This one, maybe?" She turned to him, holding up a scarf with a pattern of many colours.

"Oh, yeah. She'll like that one." He reached for it. "Now, my Mom."

"What's your mother like, Blackie?"

"She's sweet, compassionate, a neat freak but she has a wonderful sense of humour. She used to make up stories for me at bedtime and did the same for the girls. Always with a moral to them or based on a Bible story. I missed that when I grew too old for those." He watched her, compassion on his face for what she had missed. "I'm really sorry you didn't have that." His eyes raised as he felt a watcher and saw the man following them. He pulled out his phone, quickly snapping a picture and sending it off to Simon.

"He's behind me?" At his nod, she sighed. "I'll never had a normal life and I was so hopeful with you helping me get away from that house and providing me with a job."

"It will come. It may take us a bit, but we'll win your freedom from them." He tucked her arm into his and led her around the store. "Now, for Mom. She loves trinkets, collecting various objects." He stopped as she did, her hands reaching for a figurine of a mother and three children, a boy and two girls, the mother seated with a book in her hands. "Just perfect, Jewel. I would never had found that without you."

"Sure you would have. What about Finn and her mother?"

"That's a good question. What would you suggest?"

"Let's try another store. I think finding Mary something for her kitchen might work. Finn loves to read, so maybe something in that line?" She stopped. "What am I saying? You likely have your own ideas."

He shook his head. "I don't. The guys and Dad are easy to buy for. And then there's you."

Her eyes shot to his. "I don't need anything, Blackie. It's a gift enough that you got me out of that house."

He shook his head, his eyes on the man following them. "No, it's not. Come on. Let's pay for this and then ditch our shadow. Think we can?"

She stared past him. "I doubt it, but we can always try. Where are we meeting the other two?"

❄ ❄ ❄ ❄ ❄

Jacob looked up from where he had stood, waiting for Blackie to catch up with him. Finn and Julia had already gone ahead, Finn intent on finding something for Julia without her knowing it. Jacob glanced back at the store and smiled. It would be an antiquities store, he thought. Only my beloved Finn would do that. His head shot around as he heard squealing of tires and screams and searched for Blackie, not seeing him. He was torn. He needed to find Blackie, but he didn't dare leave the women on their own. This would be the perfect opportunity for someone to snatch Julia. He headed into the store, finding the women, heads bent over a selection of old-time kitchen gadgets, their laughter wafting around them.

Blackie appeared at his shoulder, brushing off his clothing.

"Blackie?" Jacob shot a look at him, then at Finn and Julia.

"Later, Jacob. Someone just tried to run me down. I'll give you the details when we're alone. Have they found anything yet?"

Jacob gave a forced laugh, his eyes on Blackie's face. "I think they have. You may need deep pockets in this store, my friend, if Finn has her way."

Blackie shook his head at Jacob's teasing. "If it loosens up Jewel more, then it's worth it." He walked up behind them, his voice so close causing them to jump. "What did you find?"

"Blackie! Look at this! Old fashioned cookie cutters! Finn says her mother would love them. What do you think?" Julia turned, her face alight with laughter and enjoyment.

"They're perfect." His eyes never left Julia's face.

"You haven't even looked at them." She shook a finger at him.

"If you like them and Finn says they'll work, then we take them." He took them, then looked around for a basket, saying a quick thanks when Jacob handed him one, watching as the two women moved away.

"Blackie, what happened?" Jacob searched the store, looking for what he wasn't sure

"We've been followed. I sent the picture of the man on to Simon. Here, this is him." He stuck his phone back into his pocket. "I think it was him that just tried to run me down out there. A quick thinking bystander pulled me out of the way in time." He looked around, finding the women just ahead of them. "We need to be very careful. It looks as if he'll do anything to get to Jewel."

"That sounds familiar, Blackie, and I don't like it. Come on. Let's stay with them."

Julia sat back, her eyes on Blackie as he watched the road around them, faintly hearing Jacob and Finn's conversation and laughter from the front seat. She reached to touch his hand, bringing him around to face her.

"What happened, Blackie? I know something did."

He sighed. "Someone tried to run me down after I put the parcels in the vehicle. I'm fine. I just didn't see who it was."

"It was likely Hal's friend. They'll try and get you out of the way, you know."

Blackie's hand turned over and he grasped hers in his. "It won't work, you know. It just won't work."

"That's what you think, but I've always heard rumours around town. Of people they've gotten rid of. People who were there one day and gone the next."

Blackie caught the look Jacob threw him and shook his head. "We'll survive, Julia. We'll make it through, no matter what we face. Together. That I promise you. I won't let you face this alone."

She shook her head, not believing him, not wanting to at any rate. She thought back to when Hal had first started to threaten anyone who helped her and knew she was fighting a losing battle with keeping Blackie safe. But what was it that Hal was trying to hide? It had to be something big for him to go to those lengths.

"Blackie, how far can we trace back my family?"

He shifted to look at her, a concerned look on his face. "Why?"

"There has to be something there that Hal wants to hide or wants to find. I have no idea what it is." She caught the look Finn gave her. "What if I'm related to one of the founding families and have something that he wants, something that would give him ownership of something or some place in town?"

"That makes weird sense, Julia." Jacob spoke up. "We can start searching tomorrow after church. I would suggest you call your dad too, Blackie, and see what help he can give."

"I'll do that tonight. I have to call anyway. Mom wants to talk to me, she says." Blackie thought back over the day and then he began to pray as he never had before. His heart lifted to God, knowing that they were facing some dark days and hours but also knowing that they wouldn't walk them alone. God had already gone before them, he knew. His eyes searched Julia's face in the darkness of the car, catching sight of it in the dimness of the light from the dashboard and the occasional flash of passing headlights. Lord, she's been through so much. She doesn't understand that You are a loving father, who loves her deeply and without end. She needs to understand that and find her place in Your family. I sense she does believe in You, has placed her trust in You already. Just walk with her through this valley and cover her with Your hand. Please, dear Lord, don't let anything happen to my lady.

Hours later, Blackie raised his head as he heard a mug set down beside him and someone move towards the desk in the study. Finn's father sank into his chair, his head in his hands for a moment before he looked up at Blackie.

"You should be in bed, Blackie. It's late."

Blackie nodded. "So should you."

Timothy gave a short laugh. "I was and couldn't sleep. That's when I get up and do some studying. I'm working through the Minor Prophets right now."

"I haven't studied those in years." Blackie hesitated, his eyes going to his laptop before he looked up to find Timothy watching him. "Timothy, you know the people in this town. Tell me about Julia's people."

"Hal has always had a very mean streak in him, all his life. He didn't get it from his parents, I can tell you that. We weren't surprised when he married Julia's mother. She's had a mean streak as well."

"She has? I can see that, but why?"

Timothy shrugged. "She wanted more than she could get in this town. Her parents wouldn't leave. She married Julia's father right after high school. Now that was a match no one saw coming. She really hid her true character from him, I would think."

"She must have." Blackie sat back. "How did her father die? She's never said."

"Car accident. But there was something strange about that. I can't remember all the details but I know there were rumours around town that he had been killed."

Blackie nodded. "That's what I was finding. The only thing I'm not finding is much of a family tree on her. It's just not there or it's hidden." He looked up at a sudden sound from Timothy and caught the distressed look on his face. "Timothy?"

"Oh my, I'm so sorry, Blackie. I had forgotten. Lord, forgive me. Her paternal grandfather and mine were cousins. That means she's family. She goes by Whittaker but that's not her name. That's Hal's."

"That also means she related to one of the founding families, yours. Did she ever legally take Hal's name, I wonder?"

"No, I never did."

Blackie shot to his feet as he spun and stared at Julia before reaching to draw her to his side and then down to the couch where he had been sitting.

"You didn't? But you go by it, don't you?"

"Not any more. I've always hated it, but he didn't give me much choice. You don't want to know the abuse I suffered until I gave in. I want my father's name back. That's the same as yours, Timothy." She hid her face against Blackie's arm. The two men shared a look before Timothy spoke.

"You're our family, Julia. I wish I had realized that before We would have gotten you out of there."

She looked up, no tears in evidence, not what they had expected. "He would have killed you or your family, Timothy. Even now, just having me here, puts you in danger."

"So, how do we mitigate that?" Blackie's mind was racing with ideas and questions. He knew there would be no sleep for him that night.

Timothy rose, heading for his filing cabinet and pulling out a folder, re-seating himself as he leafed through it. He glanced up, his keen gaze on Julia.

"Julia, how old are you?"

"Twenty-seven. The same as your Finn."

"That's what I thought. According to the old will that is honoured even today and it is legal, you had an estate coming to you when you turned twenty-five as did your brother. Did you get it?"

She shook her head. "If I had, I would have left town. What would have been the estate, Timothy?"

"I'm not sure. I can talk to my lawyer on Monday. In fact, I think you should come with me. With Finn and Peter, they got a number of buildings and stocks, bonds, and a bank account. They get more when I go. With you and your brother, Jonathan, you would split your father's. It would be similar to what I got from Dad. You don't need to worry about working, young lady, I can tell you that. You just can't sell the buildings in town."

"Wow!" Julia sat back, stunned before she turned to Blackie. "Did you know?"

He shook his head. "No, I didn't. I know Dad has an estate that he didn't know he had coming to him and he's made arrangements to split it between my sisters and I."

Julia shook her head as she stood. "I need to think this through." She walked towards the door, spinning around to find the two men standing, staring after her. "Is this what he was after, then? Dad's estate?"

"I would suspect so. He likely married your mother, thinking it came to her, and found out it didn't, that it went to you and your brother." Blackie shared a look with Timothy. "Did he ever try to get you to sign any papers around the time you turned 25?"

She stared at him, thinking through the years, and then her face paled. "He did, and I refused. They were legal looking and I just didn't feel comfortable with signing them without a lawyer explaining them to me. Is that what they were?"

"Probably. He would have tried to get your portion of the estate, but legally it would not have held up in court." Timothy watched as her face cleared. "You have nothing to worry about that way, Julia. Your father's estate from the town goes to you and your brother. It's structured in such a way to provide a perpetual income for you both."

"And Jonathan left without knowing. How do I find him? Blackie?" She turned to him, tears on her face. "This isn't it all though, is it?"

Blackie shook his head as he walked towards her. "No, I don't think it is. Neither does Simon. We're looking into Hal and his friends, trying to determine what he's all involved with."

Chapter 8

*B*lackie walked back through the town of Mistletoe, his eyes on the buildings, picking out the ones his father had said belonged to him. He smiled as he realized that Hal was paying rent to his father for his office. Now, that was something he could talk to his father about. He was sure his father would come up with something creative there to keep tabs on him.

He turned as he heard his name called and frowned, not recognizing the man walking towards him.

"You're Levi Blackwell, aren't you?" The man was tall with brown hair and brown eyes. He seemed familiar. "You don't remember me, do you?"

Blackie shook his head. "No, I'm sorry to say I don't, but I should, right?"

The man laughed and Blackie realized who it was he looked like. "Jonathan Bronagh?"

"That would be me. We met years ago on a base overseas and spent some time together. You and your three friends. Your friends who I understand are now in this town."

"They are. But you haven't been." Blackie looked around, then pointed at Josh's cafe, The House. "Josh has that cafe. We can find a booth where we can talk or he'll let us use his office."

"I would suggest his office. Less conspicuous that way. I know there's a back way in. I'll meet you there." He was gone before Blackie could say anything more.

Blackie stood for a moment, watching for anyone watching him and then headed for The House. He waved at Josh as he headed through the cafe towards Josh's office, knowing he was welcome there without a question.

He turned, closing the door behind him, and stared at the man he knew as Joe White. "Joe White's not your real name, is it?"

Jonathan shook his head. "No, it's not, and from what I understand, neither is

Jonathan Whittaker. I've been doing some research. Help me out here, Levi. I hear you've been protecting my sister."

Blackie leaned back against the door, crossing his arms and then his ankles. "How'd you hear that?"

"A friend in town. She's been watching out for Julia and let me know that you had come to town, you and your three friends. I was never so glad to hear anything as I was to hear that. I had to leave when I was 18. He'd have killed me and then killed Julia. I had to keep her alive. I've been back and forth from town over the years, making sure she's safe."

Blackie snorted. "Safe is a word I would not use for her. How many beatings could you have spared her if you had taken her with you? How much abuse?"

Jonathan paled. "He beat her? I didn't know that or I would have gotten her out of there after the first one. Why didn't someone tell me?"

"Probably because they didn't know. He's crafty, Jonathan. He's hidden what he's done. Julia is just starting to open up to me, to tell me what's been going on." He sighed as he moved to where Josh kept a coffee pot and poured himself a cup, raising the pot to Jonathan and then pouring him one as well. He sank into Josh's chair for the moment, pointing with his mug to one of the other chairs. "We need to talk and talk long and hard, Jonathan. They have already tried to kill both of us."

Jonathan's hand shook enough he had to place the mug on the corner of the desk before he buried his head into his hands. Blackie watched with compassion, realizing the other man had not known what his sister had faced. Josh cracked the door open enough to enter and then, shaking his head as Blackie went to rise, slipped into the other chair by Jonathan.

Jonathan looked up, devastation on his face. "I never knew. He used to beat me, until I finally left. I would have taken Julia with me when I left if I had ever thought." His eyes found Blackie's. "I'm guessing the letters I sent her she never got?"

Blackie shook his head before he sipped at his mug of coffee. "Not a one. She never knew where you were or I think she would have taken off to find you, somehow getting to you.”

Josh finally spoke, his words a prayer as he prayed for his friends and for Jonathan, knowing they were facing dark days ahead

They sat for a while, Josh finally having to go back to the floor. Blackie eyed the keys he was turning over and over in his hands.

“How do you want to handle this? Do you want to see Julia?”

Jonathan shook his head. “Not yet. I need to get a better handle on what Hal has been up to.”

Blackie gave a bark of laughter, causing Jonathan to stare at him. “Sorry. I was just thinking of how Julia’s going to react when she finds out you’ve been in town and not gone to find her. I don’t want to be the one who tells her that.”

Jonathan stared at him for a moment longer. “How serious are you?”

“Very, but that’s something I discuss with Julia first. She deserves that.”

Jonathan nodded. "I agree. Now, I need to get out of here. Here's my cell number. Call me if you need me. I'll be around town somewhere."

"Before you go, here's my Dad's number. Call him and talk to him. He'll want what you know. He's been looking into this town for about a month and finding some interesting items he hasn't shared with me yet."

Jonathan took the card, programmed in the number and then handed it back. "It's better I not have that on me. No one can get into my phone but me." He looked at Blackie for a moment. "I know your father, have talked to him over the years. He has never said but I have done work for him before. That's what I'm up to right now, why I'm back here. Not to keep an eye on you. He assures me you can take care of yourself, but I wonder, now that you told me Hal tried to kill Julia and I suspect you were involved in that." He held up a hand. "Don't tell me. I'll find you when I need." With that he was gone, leaving Blackie staring at the doorway, surprised when he saw Jacob and Simon standing in it behind Josh.

"Called in reinforcements, did you?" Blackie moved away from the desk, back towards the coffee pot, before he stared down at his mug and set it down. "We have a problem, guys, and I have no idea what the solution is."

"Talk to us, Blackie. That's how we resolve things." Simon shoved the door closed. "Can we talk here, Josh, or do we need to move to somewhere more private?"

"I would say we meet tonight and talk. I'm going to be on and off the floor all day. How about my place around 7?"

Blackie found Julia later that afternoon, curled up in a chair in the family living room, her eyes on a book, but he could tell she wasn't reading it. He slid down into a chair near her and waited. She finally looked up, a smile growing on her face.

"I didn't hear you come in, Blackie."

"I just got here. I don't think you were reading though, were you?"

She shook her head. "I've had too much to think about, I guess. Have you talked to your father?"

"I did. He confirms what Timothy said, that your Dad's share would have gone to you. The buildings are shared between you as is the bank account. Your mother didn't get anything from the estate at all. Your father left everything, including his life insurance, to you and your brother."

"So, if Hal thought he was getting a fortune by marrying Mom, he didn't." Her eyes strayed to the window, not seeing the wreath hanging in it. "That would explain why he's been like that with me. I just wish I knew for sure if that's why."

Blackie reached to draw her to her feet and into his arms. He felt her relax against him and then her arms came around him, under the plaid flannel shirt he was wearing as a jacket. Her head came down on his chest even as he tightened his hold on her.

"He's playing mind games with you, Jewel, trying to wear you down. We won't let him win. I promise you that. I will do everything in my power to keep you safe."

Her head came back so she could look up at him. "I know you will and that scares me, Blackie. I don't want you hurt and he will hurt you if he can, particularly if he knows you're important to me."

"And am I?" He watched as she nodded. "I'm so glad, Jewel. You're so important to me, important enough for me to take a chance and ask that you be my best girl for life. I love you. I also believe in love at first sight. Will you?"

She moved back a bit more, her eyes on his, her mouth rounded in surprise, before her features softened and she nodded. "If you'll be my best beau, as my Dad used to say."

"That's good enough for now. We'll talk more as we go along." His head bent as he kissed her gently, the first kiss leading to another and another.

A chuckle rang through the room and Julia felt Blackie's body start to shake in laughter even as he raised his head to smile at her.

"Really, Levi?" A male voice had a tinge of laughter in it.

"Yes, Dad. Now go away. Let me kiss my best girl in peace."

Shocked, Julia stared at him, even as he shook his head and kissed her again. Moving back a bit, he whispered, "It's okay. It's my father. We'll be getting some teasing, I suspect."

"He lets you talk to him that way?"

Mischief sparkled on Blackie's face. "He does, within reason and with respect." He groaned as he heard a teenager's voice.

"Levi? What are you doing?" The words were cut off abruptly as the speaker protested having her eyes covered and then there was silence.

"You're too young to see this, Rebecca." They heard a squeal of protest from the second speaker even as laughter rang out again and the voice was silenced.

"And so are you, Rachel."

"Samuel, behave yourself. Take your hands off Rachel's eyes and mouth. Rachel, you do the same for your sister. Girls, Mary has something for you in the kitchen. Your brother will be out shortly to see you. Behave yourselves now." Laughter tinged the woman's voice.

Julia stared at Blackie as he began to laugh harder and swept her back into a hug. "It's okay. My family's here. A surprise or I would have warned you."

"You would have warned me?" Julia hugged him tight. "Do you know how long I have prayed for a family like yours? For Jonathan and I?" Tears sparkled on her lashes as he hugged her back.

A warm hand rubbing along his back had him turning, his arm still around Julia even as he stooped to give his mother a kiss on the cheek and reach to shake his father's hand. Samuel took one look at Julia and then nodded. Thank you, Lord. She's what he needs. I don't understand how You bring people together but You do.

Miriam greeted her son, and then stood, hand on his arm for a moment before her hands came up to cover her mouth in a surprised gesture and tears brimmed in her eyes. Samuel's arm was around her shoulder as she stared first at Julia and then up at her oh so tall son. When did he grow up on me, Lord, she asked? It just seems like yesterday I was tucking a toddler into bed and here he is, on the brink of starting a life of his own in a new way.

Blackie stood watching his mother, a smile on his face, seeing the look Julia was shifting between mother and son.

"You found her, Levi. I really didn't think she existed. But she does and you really did find her."

"I did, Mom. I really did." He took pity on Julia and hugged her tighter to him. "Mom used to make up stories for us at bedtime. Did I tell you that? I can't remember. Mine were of valiant knights and men of honour. There was also a lady in them, a beautiful lady. The knight and the lady would fall in love after he rescued her from some predicament." He stopped, sharing a look with his mother. Then a beautiful smile broke on his face. "She described you, Julia. Almost perfectly."

She was shaking her head by the time he finished. "She can't have. It's just not possible. We've never met before." Her words were almost panicked, her eyes flying to Miriam.

"It's true, Julia. It is so true. God was in that, preparing us for you, for us to welcome you to our family." She reached to hug the younger woman, who clung to her as sobs shook her body. Miriam's arms tightened around her, hugging her as only a loving mother could.

Samuel drew his son away. "Let the women be for now, son. She's perfect for you, I can see that." He nodded towards the kitchen. "She won't have a moment of peace once the girls get a hold of her."

Blackie gave a short laugh. "I know. I need to prepare her for that."

"Don't. Let her find her way with them. Your mom will keep the girls in line." He looked back. "I'm glad you found her, you know." He turned back to Blackie. "You haven't asked yet why we're here."

Blackie started to laugh harder at that. "I really haven't had a chance, now have I, Dad? Why are you here?"

Samuel laughed with his son. "Let's find us some coffee and Timothy. He said you'd tell me where his study was."

"That I can do." He stopped before he reached the kitchen. "Do I really have to go in there?"

Samuel laughed hard at that, slapping his son on his shoulder as he moved past him. "You do. The girls have been anxious to see their big brother."

Blackie took a moment to absorb what had just passed, thanking God that Julia had been receptive to his question. His eyes slid shut for a moment, popping open when he heard his name said from in front of him. He reached to hug Rebecca.

"When did you grow up, Rebecca?"

She laughed at him. "When you've been away. Was that Julia?" She looked up at him, similar eyes and features to his staring back at him.

"That she is, squirt. That she is. Now, do we have coffee and cookies, or did you drink all the coffee and eat all Mary's cookies?" He wrapped her into another hug, reaching for Rachel as she appeared in the doorway, heading for her brother.

"Levi? Who was that?" She hugged her brother tight. They were best buddies when together and she feared someone taking her place with him.

"That's Julia, love." He sent Rebecca back to the kitchen, but Rebecca kept shooting glances over her shoulder until she was out of sight. Then his attention turned to Rachel and he drew her away from the doorway. "As I said, that's Julia. She's special to me, Rachel. Do you remember the stories Mom used to make up for us?" When she nodded, he continued, "She's the lady in mine. But no one will come between you and I. Life will change for us. It already has, Rachel, but you are my sister and very precious to me. Do you understand?"

She nodded. "I do, Levi. I really do. I can't wait to meet her." She moved to walk past him but he stopped her. She frowned at him.

"Let Mom have a chance to talk to her. She's had a really rotten life so far, her mother has not been like our Mom. Let's share ours with her for a bit."

She shrugged. "Sure. Whatever. Mary has the best cookies, you know?" She linked her arm with his and drew him laughing to the kitchen.

Chapter 9

Blackie watched his father pace Timothy's study later that day. He hadn't made it to meet with his friends but they had willingly come to meet at the B&B. They were glad to see Samuel, always glad for his teasing and his words of wisdom.

Simon finally spoke from where he stood, arm on the mantle, eyes on the fire burning in the fireplace. "Josh says you met someone today, Blackie."

Blackie nodded, his eyes on his father, who had stopped and turned to face him, nodding at his son before Blackie spoke. "We did. Julia's brother." He shot a quick glance at the closed door, the first time he had seen it closed since he had come to stay there. "He says he knows you, Dad."

"He does. I really didn't know he was from here. I had Stephen research him and approve him for employment with us. You know me. Where someone comes from is not the important thing. It's who they are."

Blackie agreed with his father but was puzzled. "He said you had him watching people in this town. Not on our account, though."

"That's correct, son. I can't say much as the investigation was handed to me as a confidential one, my eyes only and only those who I chose to bring in know some of what I know. Jonathan didn't tell me he was from here but he has been invaluable to the investigation because of that." Samuel stopped, his eyes on Timothy. "You've been in our church at home, Timothy. You spoke at a men's retreat once."

Timothy nodded. "I did. I had the privilege of sharing a dinner table with you, Samuel. I never knew we'd meet again this way, or that our families would be connected in this way."

Samuel smiled. "God works in ways we never understand. I think He laid the burden for this town on my heart that day. I have prayed for you and this town since then."

Timothy nodded once again. "Of course you have. You have been in my prayers as well. Now, where do we stand?"

They stared at Blackie as he suddenly laughed, mirth brimming in his eyes. "Sorry. I just remembered something." He turned to his father. "Julia's stepfather, Hal Whittaker? He rents office space in one of the buildings you own."

Samuel grinned. "He does? Wonderful. I think there's an empty office right beside his, if I remember correctly. I didn't know that was him though when the lease came up for renewal two months ago." He shook a finger at Blackie. "No, we don't. We can just not renew in when it comes up in ten months."

Blackie grinned at his father. "Maybe it won't take that long." He sobered, eyes on his friends. "So, what have you all come up with?"

Josh spoke first. "I've had feelers out about Hal's businesses. They are all illegal - drugs, gambling, protection money. I can't say if it's gone any further, but people aren't talking a lot about him. They're running scared. He has a vicious group working for him."

"And how much did they demand from you?" Timothy spoke up, knowing

Josh would have been approached as a newcomer to town.

"Enough that I would have had to shut down the cafe and that would seem to be their plan. Shut it down, take it over, and open it up again." Josh shook his head. "I hear rumours this is what he's done over the years."

"I've heard the same rumours. He tried that with me years ago, but he quickly learned he had approached the wrong man." Timothy sat back in his chair, his eyes on Blackie. "Blackie, what more has Julia had to say about what's been going on?"

"Not a lot, Timothy. I think she's buried it all way down inside her and I don't know if it will ever all come to the surface or if it does it will come in one great rush. That's what I'm afraid of. I think she's seen or heard something she shouldn't have heard." He paused, his thoughts on his lady, wondering just how to reach her. "She needs a lot of prayer, Timothy. She really does."

"We are doing just that for her, son." Blackie looked up at his father as he sat on the couch beside him, his hand going to his son's shoulder. "Your Mom will reach her. She has that knack of pulling things out that people can't or won't share. Just stay close to your lady."

"She will. Rachel and Rebecca will do her good. I could hear the four of the ladies giggling from the girls' room. I have no idea what they're planning but I'm sure we'll be in trouble, Jacob."

"Only a quarter of as much as you will be." Jacob smirked at it took Blackie a minute to figure out what he meant. The other men laughed at Blackie's expense even as he grinned at Jacob.

"So now what, Dad? Simon? Where do we go from here? I'm out of my league here. This is nowhere what I am used to."

"We wait. We investigate. I'm learning more and more about Hal every day, Blackie." Simon looked at Samuel, who nodded. "I'm not even sure if Hal Whittaker is his right name."

"And if it's not, then who is he?"

"That the question we're trying to answer. Leave it with us for a few more days. Stay close to Julia. Don't let her out of your sight when you are away from here. If needed, my supervisor has agreed to pull some officers from here and put her into a protective custody situation.”

Blackie shook his head. “She’ll never go for that, Simon. Not after how she lived all her life. She’s tasted freedom and wants to stay that way. Even a day would break her again. And I won’t have that.”

Simon nodded. “I get that, Blackie. We all do, but we have to consider that might be a possibility, even for a few days. I pray it isn’t.” He looked at the clock. “I need to leave. I’m on call starting at midnight and need to catch as much sleep as I can.” Simon walked away, leaving Josh to follow shortly after him. The four remaining men sat in quiet until Mary came looking for Timothy.

“Timothy, James is on the phone. Something about the worship team for tomorrow not being available due to illness?”

“On it, love.” He walked away, his arm around his wife, leaving Jacob to follow after him looking for Finn.

Samuel studied his son for a few minutes, seeing how lost in thought he was. His hand tightened on Blackie's shoulder, drawing Blackie's attention to him.

"Dad, where do I go from here with Jewel? She's not used to living like you raised us. I know that's going to create issues."

"It may and it may not. Be open to her. Let her have her privacy and her space if she needs it. Let her know you understand she's hurting and broken and needs God to heal her. Pray for her and with her. That's the important one, Levi. Pray with her. I know your heart is entangled now but don't lose sight of how much she needs healing and shelter that only God can provide." He paused, not quite sure how to proceed. "I get the sense that you're not quite satisfied working for me."

Blackie looked at his father. "I am, Dad. I love working with you, but there's something I feel I should be doing. Some kind of ministry. There are kids here out on the streets after school and on weekends that have no place to hang around."

"Well, you do have your psychology diploma. You did manage to get that while in the service. Use it here. Take one of our buildings, fix it up as a youth centre. I'll take to the town council for you. Give me a business plan and a diagram for what you plan to do. Tomorrow's Sunday, but we can walk through town, and see which building would suit."

"Thanks, Dad. I'll plan on that." Saying good night to his father, he walked through the door to find Julia standing just outside the door, not wanting to disturb the men. "You could have come in, Julia. We don't bite."

She smiled at him as he took her hand. "I know, but you haven't seen your dad in a bit."

"That's not the point. If you're going to be part of our lives, and I pray you will, he'll welcome you to any conversation we're involved in, unless it's a private one. Those he pulls us aside into a room with a closed door and talks. He always has."

She nodded, stopping suddenly in the hallway. Blackie reached to hug her, finding her stiff and unresponsive.

"Julia? Julia, what's wrong?"

She didn't respond and he swept her into his arms heading for her room, calling for his mother as he went. Miriam and Mary ran behind him up the stairs, watching as he laid her on her bed and then began assessing her.

"Levi?"

"Don't know, Mom. She all of a sudden went stiff and hasn't responded. Mary, do you know a doctor who will come and see her?"

"I do. From the church. Levi, come with me. Let your Mom get her settled and then we'll come back. I want you to talk to Allan. You can tell him what happened."

He followed Mary from the room, taking the phone from her as she put in the call to their friend from church and describing rapidly what had happened. He breathed a sigh of relief when Allan gave him some directions and offered to come over if needed, and then handed Mary the phone as he heard Miriam calling quietly for him.

"Mom?" He stood in front of her, eyes search her face.

"She's awake, Levi. I can't get her to settle into bed. She just won't." Tears sparkled in his mother's eyes in the dim light. "Oh, Levi, son! What has he done to her?"

"What do you mean, Mom?" He was getting scared, not knowing what his mother was talking about.

"I helped her into a fleece suit, Levi. That's what she wanted. Her back is scarred, Levi. She flinched when I lightly touched her."

Blackie hugged his mother. "She was abused, Mom, by her stepfather and either no one knew or no one did anything. Let me talk with her." He paused, his hands lightly resting on his mother's arms. "She needs a mother, Mom, just like you. Hers wasn't. Thank you." He moved past her to stop in the bedroom doorway, watching Julia pace the floor.

Julia heard a slight noise and spun, fear on her face that vanished when she saw

Blackie.   She launched herself at him, feeling safe in his arms.

"Jewel?   Can you tell me what happened?"   His voice was kept low and calm, even though his heart was racing with fear and concern.

She finally nodded. "I can. Can we go downstairs? I need to be on a first floor tonight."

"We can do that." He swept her into his arms and carried her back down to the dimly light living room area, settling down into a chair and cradling her close. "Do you want to talk about what happened?"

"In a bit. Just let me be for a few minutes." Her head nestled down on his shoulder as she stared straight ahead.

Blackie felt hands on his back tucking a blanket around his shoulders and then a blanket was tucked over Julia. His mother dropped a kiss on his head before she moved away. He heard quiet voices and then felt his father's arms around them both, his voice sounding out quietly in prayer for them before he too left.

Finally, Julia's head tipped back and she looked up at him. "Thank you, Blackie. Everyone else would have tried to make me talk right away."

"You weren't ready. You would have just shut down even further if I tried to force it."

"You're right. I would have." She sighed. "Do I have to leave my town to get peace?"

"No, you don't. God will grant you His peace right here and now. It's yours for the asking. But talk to me. Tell me what happened."

She shuddered. "He heard that the descendants of the original settlers were coming back. He plans to kill all of you and take over the town." She tilted her head back to look up at him.

"That's not going to happen. First, he's not going to kill us. Secondly, he can never take over the town. It just can't happen. The founders made sure of that." His arms tightened around her. "Now, what else did you remember?"

"How did you know I did?"

He shrugged. "I don't know, love. I just do. And it's not because of the psychology diploma I have."

"You're analyzing me?" She pushed to get away, but wasn't able to loosen his arms enough to do so. Anger settled on her face.

"No, I'm not. I would never do that to you. I had to do something with my spare time and that's what I did. I wasn't even sure I would ever use it. So you're safe with me."

She shook her head before she calmed down. "Just make sure you never do." Her eyes stared towards the closed windows. "Do you think someone is out there, prowling around, trying to get to us?"

Blackie shrugged. "There might be, but I doubt it."

They talked for a while longer before her head went down on his shoulder and she slept. He tugged the blanket up higher over her and settled back himself, his head resting lightly against hers, his heart raised in petition to God for peace and safety for his beloved.

Chapter 10

*B*lackie looked up the next morning, raising his head from his Bible as he heard footsteps stop outside his bedroom door and then a light tap at the door. He rose, looking longingly back at the passage he was reading before he opened the door to find his youngest sister standing there. He stepped back, letting her in.

Rebecca's arms hugged her brother and then held on, not willing to let him go.

"Rebecca? What's the problem?" Blackie gently stepped back, a hand on his sister's cheek.

"I don't want you to get hurt."

"And who says I will?"

"I heard Mom and Dad talking. Dad doesn't want to leave you here on your own."

"Rebecca, what did we talk about when I went into the forces? Didn't we say God was in control and only He could really protect me?" When she nodded, he continued, "It's the very same right now. God is in control. He will protect."

She finally turned to the door. "I know that in my head, Levi, but I can't convince my heart of that." She faced him again. "Please stay safe. Mom says Rachel, she and I are heading home tomorrow for a few days but that Dad's staying. Is that true?"

"I have no idea, Rebecca. I haven't talked to them this morning." He watched as the door closed, sighing to himself. I need this over with, Lord, and soon. All of my loved ones are hurting.

Blackie turned as his father approached him later that afternoon. They had spent the morning in a worship service that both challenged and calmed them, Blackie though, if those words could be used in the same sentence.

"Blackie, I've asked your Mom to take the girls home for the week. They have to finish their classes before the Christmas break, and then they'll be back here for the following weeks. I'm at the point in my investigation that I need to be here in town."

"Rebecca's a little put out that she has to go home, you know." Blackie grinned as he remembered the look on her face.

"I know she is, but it's necessary. And no, I'm not staying because you're in trouble, but I sense that what you two are facing is all tied up in what I've been asked to determine." Samuel paced, wanting to share more openly with his son, but constrained from doing so by the confidentiality agreement he had signed.

"Listen, Dad, I know you can't talk about it. That's fine. But I do have a question for you." Samuel had turned to face Blackie as he spoke. "Can we go for one of our walks? I would like to take a look at some of those buildings you own."

Ten minutes later, the men approached the first of the buildings and circled it, coming back to stand staring up at it.

"It's in good shape. I thought it would be more rundown." Samuel reached his pockets, coming up with a key. "I brought keys with me this weekend, hoping to look through some of the buildings."

Blackie followed his father through the first floor, liking what he saw. "This is great, Dad. It's got great bones. It would make a good youth centre. The rooms are large, so we wouldn't have to knock down any walls."

"Let's check upstairs. Of all the buildings, I think this is the one that would suit you best."

They finally returned to the first floor, Samuel watching his son closely and knowing his thoughts were not totally on the building. "Talk to me, son. What's really going on?"

Blackie shook his head. "I'm really not sure, Dad. It's all this with Jewel. I know Hal isn't finished with her yet and that her life is likely in danger. I just want to protect her, but I need to let her have the freedom she's never had. Even if it means she walks away from me." He blinked rapidly at that thought.

"Love hurts, son. That's what happens when we care so much. I almost lost your Mom before you were born." Blackie's head shot around. He had never heard that. "She was really sick. The doctors never did figure out what it was, but they only gave us a couple of days for her to survive. Our church prayed, hands were laid on her and she was anointed. She rallied and survived."

"Is that why she has to take care when she's around someone that's really sick?"

Samuel nodded. "It is. Since we don't know the trigger, we can't prevent it from happening again. Now, about you four boys. What can I do to help you with your investigation? And I know you are. You've told me what transpired with Jacob."

Blackie nodded. "I will, Dad, but can we go back to the B&B? I feel unsafe here today, for some reason, and I shouldn't."

Samuel searched his son's face and then nodded. "We can. I have that same feeling. How was Julia this morning?"

"She seemed okay, embarrassed at what happened last night. I don't think she realizes Mom saw her scars."

Samuel's steps slowed and stopped even as his hand came out to stop Blackie's forward motion. "Scars? What are you talking about?"

Blackie looked at his father, shock on his face. "Mom didn't tell you? Hal beat Julia and she has the scars to show for it." He paused, a thought crossing his mind. "Just how far will he go to get possession of their inheritance?"

"As far as he can, likely. Money and power drive some people to do unconscionable things. And I think he's one of them."

Blackie turned and headed for the B&B, almost on a run, his father on his heels. "Finn and her family are gone for the day. Mary said all the guests were headed out. The girls have gone to a youth event at the church. That leaves Mom and Jewel on their own."

Blackie ran through the B&B, desperately searching for his mother and Julia. Hearing a sound from off the kitchen, he tried to open the pantry door, finding it stuck and not able to move it. Samuel lent his weight but it still didn't budge.

"Miriam, are you in there?"

"Samuel? We are. Wait. I have to move some stuff. You can't open the door.

We barricaded ourselves in here." The door finally flew open and the women emerged.

Samuel caught his wife in his arms, not caring about anything but that she was fine. Disheveled, but fine.

Blackie stood for a moment, seeing the fear on Julia's face before she ran the few feet separating them to throw herself at him. He caught her, feeling the shudders shaking her body. He wrapped her tight in his arms, finally turning and pulling out a chair to sit and cradle her close.

"Jewel? What happened?"

"They came looking for me, Blackie. They tried to take me with them but your mother hit them with something. I can't remember what." She leaned around Blackie to look at Miriam. "What did you use again?"

Miriam started to laugh. "First the broom and that broke. Then the vacuum hose until they grabbed it from me. By that time, I had you in the pantry. I think… Now what did I grab up?"

Samuel straightened up from picking an object up off the floor, trying to control the laughter that threatened to break out. "This?"

"That? That whatever it is?" Miriam stared at him in shock as he held up something she couldn't put a name to. "I have no idea what that is. Do you?"

Finn had entered the room without them hearing her. "You mean the old-fashioned corn popper? You defended yourself with that?"

"I guess I must have. It kept them away long enough to shut the door." She looked up at Finn and then past her at Mary. "I'm sorry, Mary. I think I made a mess of your organized pantry."

By this time, the men had open smiles on their faces, barely controlling their laughter. Finn was not as generous. She was bent almost double as gales of laughter pealed from her and she had to wipe her eyes. "Oh, I would have loved to have seen that. I never knew you could use that for a defence weapon."

Miriam shared a look with Julia even as she smirked. "Well, now you know. It's very useful. Know where we can get some more to carry with us?"

That sent the men off in fresh peals of laughter, imagining the four women walking down the street, each carrying a long-handled corn popper.

Blackie finally sobered enough to look Julia over, satisfying himself she was fine. "Who was it, Jewel?"

"Hal's cronies. One was the man from yesterday, who followed us." She held up her wrist and anger burned through him at the red fingermarks that showed. "When your mother hit him with the broom, he let go of me." She paused, wonder coming over her face. "He really does, doesn't He?"

"Who really does, love?" Blackie had an idea of what she was going to say but waited.

"God! He really does protect us, doesn't He? He must have sent your parents here this weekend. If your mother hadn't been here with your dad, I would have been on my own. I don't think I could have protected myself that well."

Blackie breathed a sigh of relief and wonder. Thank you, Lord. You're working there, showing her You really do care.

"He does, Jewel. About everything. I'm so glad you're realizing it. It doesn't mean we won't have trouble or face danger, but He has promised us He's there. When we seek Him, He will be found. That is a treasure you will never lose."

She nodded. "I'm finally getting what you've been saying. Your youngest sister helped me to see that."

"Rebecca? How?"

"She remembers how she felt when you went off the first time and she didn't know if she'd see you again. She said she tried praying but didn't think she was getting through to God. Then one day she found a little sparrow on the ground. It let her approach it and pick it up and hold it for a few minutes before it flew off. She quoted that verse about how much more important we are to God than even a sparrow." She glanced at him, finding his eyes fixed on her face. "That got through to me. No one else ever has, but your sister did. She's so precious, Blackie. We need to keep her here."

"Ssh. Don't tell her that, or she'll never leave."

❊ ❊ ❊ ❊ ❊ ❊

Blackie looked around the building he had decided would work as his youth centre and sighed. It was the next day and he was on his own. Today, it didn't look so bright for him to design this. Yesterday, he had been full of plans and dreams. Until that is he got home and found out what had happened to Julia and his mother. That scared him. It angered him as well and that was something he was working on leaving with God.

He paced through the building, his mind finally on the decisions he needed to make. His father had told him to do what he wanted with the place, he'd fund it. He knew friends who would be glad to chip in as well. His father was already working on a business plan for him and setting up a trust fund and board of directors for him. Things Blackie hadn't even had a chance to think about, and he was glad his father had taken that step. Samuel wasn't trying to take over but he knew that Blackie's mind wasn't on that part of the plan yet. He would make no decisions without Blackie's input, that he had guaranteed Blackie.

Blackie heard a whisper of sound behind him as he turned from the kitchen area and felt the blow to his back, driving him to his knees. He came up, facing around to his assailant.

"It's you, is it?" The man who had followed them on Saturday stood in front of him, a pipe in one hand, a sharp long-bladed knife in the other. "Which are you planning on using on me? The pipe or the knife? I hear you didn't fare that well with Mom."

"She's lucky." The man's voice was guttural, as if he was hiding the real sound of it. "You won't be."

Blackie circled around, trying to remember how far it was to the front door, and praying he'd have time to reach it and get through it before the man attacked. His eyes fastened on the man's face, watching for the slightly movement that would show him which way the man planned to go.

The man lunged at Blackie, who deflected the hand with the knife and then ducked the swing of the pipe. Blackie knew he had to get the man to drop one or the other of the weapons but wasn't quite sure how.

A misstep on his part had him sliding sideways, the pipe crashing down on his shoulder and sending him to his knees. He reached for the pipe, leaving his abdomen open to attack. He felt the knife as it sliced into him and he dropped to the floor, hands reaching for the wound even as the man knelt on his chest and leaned close, telling him he was done for and that they'd have Julia now. No one could protect her. And that as one of the founding family descendants, he would be the first of his family to die, leaving it open to them to take over the funds.

Blackie's vision blurred and swirled as he sank into darkness, blood dripping to the floor. He lost sight of the man and didn't feel the shove on his chest from the knee as the man rose and then stood over him, glee on his face, as he thought he had won.

Fifteen minutes later, Jacob and Finn came looking for Blackie. He had failed to show up at the cafe as promised and they were afraid, afraid something had happened to him.

Jacob had stopped to search in one of the rooms when he heard a cry from Finn and ran to where she stood, hands to her face, before he rushed past her to drop to his knees beside Blackie, hands reaching for him, even as he yelled over his shoulder for Finn to call for help.

Hands shaking, he rolled Blackie over onto his back and reached to tear away his jacket and then the flannel shirt and T-shirt. He gave a cry and took the scarf Finn handed him, shoving it against the wound, desperately trying to stem the flow of blood.

"Check his pulse and breathing, Finn. I need to know he's still alive."

Finn dropped on the other side of Blackie, hands reaching of his chest and then his neck. "He's still breathing, but it's so shallow. His pulse is very slow." She looked up at Jacob, horror and hope intermingled. "Will he live?"

"I pray he does. Watch for the paramedics, Finn. We need to get him out of here. Call Josh or Simon. One of them was going to be with Samuel today. Warn them to bring him to the hospital. And to bring Julia. He needs her there. Blackie dropped hints last night that they had come to an agreement, but he didn't say to what."

She nodded as she rose, phone in hand, and ran for the door, hearing the sounds of the sirens screaming through the air and then the shrill screeching of brakes as the emergency vehicles slid to a stop.

"In here! He's been stabbed! We're not sure how long ago." Finn pointed to where Jacob has still on his knees, hands pressing against the wound. Then she heard Simon's voice in her ear and turned away, sobs wracking through her voice to the point she could hardly tell him what had happened

❄ ❄ ❄ ❄ ❄ ❄

Samuel ran through the doors to the Emergency Room at the Merryville Hospital, looking for his son's friends. Jacob was there, drawing him aside. Samuel saw Finn sitting with her arm around Julia. Good, was all he could think.

"Jacob?"

"He's alive. Samuel. They're assessing him now but are heading to surgery with him right away. He was stabbed in the abdomen, how severe they haven't said yet. The physician will be out shortly. They know you were on your way."

"I have to call Miriam. This is not something I want to tell her over the phone."

"Simon called the police department in your town. He found a friend working there who will take your pastor with him to go tell her. If that helps?"

Samuel gave a sigh of relief. "It will, but I still need to talk to her." He nodded towards the women. "How's Julia?"

"In shock." Jacob turned to stare at her. "How serious are those two?"

"Serious enough that Levi asked for his grandmother's ring to come back with his mother on Friday."

"Wow! I didn't think it had gone that far." Jacob turned as he heard steps behind them. "Here's the physician, Samuel."

Julia rose and was at Samuel's side before the physician had reached him. His arm came around the lady he know would be his daughter-in-law. That is, if his son survived.

"Doctor?"

"He's alive and very lucky. The thick jacket helped to slow the knife and kept it from going as deep as it should have. We're taking him up to surgery to repair it. We'll assess if there is any further internal damage, but from my look, I don't think there is. Someone was watching out for you son, Mr. Blackwell."

"God was, Doctor. Now, can we see him before he goes to surgery?"

The physician nodded, looking askance at Julia.

"This is his fiancee, Doctor. She's going in."

Julia stared up at Samuel, dumbfounded at his words, but he shook his head at her.

"We'll talk later, Julia, but I know that's what Levi is thinking, isn't it?"

She gave an abrupt nod, then followed the nurse along the hallway, stopping for a moment at the curtain before Samuel's gentle hand on her back urged her forward.

She paused, her eyes going up to Samuel's, finding him whispering a prayer even as she stood, waiting, not sure what she'd find in the room. She finally moved forward to where the nurse was waiting, her eyes seeking Blackie.

She stood, one hand on Blackie's cheek, the other on his arm as she studied him, seeing the paleness of his face, before her eyes raised and traced the IV lines and other lines running to him. She watched the monitors, a frown on her face as she realized she really didn't understand them. Samuel stood beside her, an arm around her, his hand on Blackie's shoulder. She could hear his whispered prayer once more.

Blackie's movements stilled as he felt Julia's hand on his face, and his eyes flickered open. He strained to focus, finding first his father's face.

"Dad?"

"It's fine, son. You're in the hospital."

"It hurts." His hands shoved at the blankets before Julia's hands reached to stop him. "What happened?"

"You were hurt, son. Now, they'll need to take you to surgery."

"No, I need to get up and out of here." He struggled to rise, his hands shoving once more against the blankets and then fumbling at the side rail of the bed.

"Stay put, son. They'll be coming for you soon."

Blackie's head went back and his eyes slid closed. "I can't. You don't understand, Dad. I need to find Jewel. They'll be after her. He threatened her."

Samuel's eyes found Julia's, seeing the fear lurking in hers. "Who threatened her?"

"I don't know his name. He's been following us. He's going to come and get her. I need to find her and save her."

Julia's hands reached for his, clasping his tightly. "I'm right here, Blackie. I'm safe."

"Jewel? You're safe? But he said they were coming for you." Blackie's eyes flickered open, he looked up at her, and then his eyes slid closed again as he lost the fight to keep conscious.

Samuel drew Julia away as the nurses approached, ready to head off with Blackie. Julia stood, hands to her mouth, eyes sparkling with the tears she refused to shed, before she turned into Samuel's hug. He gently led her to the waiting room and then followed Simon to the surgical waiting area, seating her and then turning to Simon.

"Levi was awake, Simon." Samuel had moved away from where Julia sat, Finn and Jacob on either side of her. "He didn't see Julia at first and tried to get up to find her. He said whoever attacked him was after her and he thought they had her already."

Simon paused his hand as he lifted the cup of coffee to his mouth, his eyes on Julia. "Did he recognize the man?"

"He said he had been following them? I hadn't heard that." Samuel ran his hand through his hair, pulling it back as he stared at it, willing it to stop shaking. "I never felt like this when he was in the service, but today? I could have lost him, Simon, so easily, with me right in the same town."

"God was watching out for him, Samuel, that you can depend on." Simon turned as he heard footsteps and saw Josh approaching. "Josh? Who's minding the cafe?"

"I called in extra help for the next two weeks. I want in on this, Simon, and if you say no, then I work on my own. Someone pulled us all back to this town. Jacob went through something. Blackie is in the midst of something and could have easily died. We need to find out who is back of this, because I can guarantee you he's not finished. You and I will be next, don't you think?" Josh stood, hands jammed into his pockets, staring around, determination flowing from him.

"Simon, I know who he meant." Simon looked up to see Julia standing at the edge of their group. "It's Hal's best friend. He's the one who has been following us. I think he's likely the one Hal used for doing whatever he needed done. Hal would keep his hands clean, except where it came to Jonathan or I. He let Benny do the dirty work." Her voice faded away for a moment. "Samuel, did you say you own that building?" At his nod, she sighed. "I think

134

if you look either in the basement or in the attic, you'll find some evidence you need. But I wouldn't wait too long, or it will be gone. I vaguely remember Hal and Mom talking about something like that." Her voice faded once more as she stared past the men, then brushing by them, walked into the hallway and towards the elevators. "Jonathan?" Her voice was quiet, so quiet they weren't sure they had heard her right.

The man turned, his eyes on the men before they fell to Julia. Julia stopped for a moment before she began to run, throwing herself at the man, whose arms swept her into a tight hug.

"Julia, you shouldn't be out here. I didn't mean for you to see me. Not yet."

Simon had been right behind Julia, sweeping Julia and Jonathan into an empty room and closing the door behind them, standing guard outside.

Julia clung to her brother, sobs wracking her body. Jonathan's own tears flowed, holding his sister after so many years. He finally released her enough that he could step back and see her face.

"Julia? Look at me." When she did, he winced, seeing the pain and sorrow on her face. "I'm so sorry, Julia. I should have taken you with me when I went but I had no money, nothing for us to survive on. I tried coming back a few years ago but Benny found me and beat me up, dumping me miles away. I've had someone watching you, though."

Julia hit at his shoulders with her closed fists. "Not close enough, Jonathan. No where near close enough. Do you know how many beatings I took over the years?"

Jonathan froze, realizing for the first time the real danger she had been in. "Oh, Julia! If I had only known."

"No one knew. That's the thing. No one knew. He made sure they didn't." She watched her brother's face, seeing the conflicting emotions crossing it. "Did you ever know we are related to the Bronaghs that have the B&B? As in cousins? Our grandfathers were cousins."

"That is our last name, but I didn't realize we were related that close." He groaned. "That's why he's after us. We're part of the legacy of the founding families."

He turned to pace. "I don't like this, Julia. Not at all. That's why Hal has been like he is. He wants what we have."

"But he can't get it. Samuel and Timothy have been checked into it. He will never get it. If one of the founding families die out, their portion goes into trust for the other four."

A tap at the door interrupted them, and Simon slipped into the room.

"The nurse is looking for you, Julia. Blackie's in recovery but not cooperating with them. He wants to get up to find you. The surgeon has asked that you come there and calm your boyfriend down." Simon grinned at the frown she threw him. As she started for the door, his hand on her arm stopped her. "I'm going with you. I know the nurse but we're not taking any chances. For now, someone is with you. At least until we find these guys."

She shook her head. "That can't happen, Simon. You can't pull your men to do that."

"We're not. Samuel has called in people."

"Samuel? But why?"

Jonathan shared a look with Simon before he nodded. "Because to him, you're family and he takes care of his family. Now, let Simon take you to Blackie.   I'll be around, sis. I'm not walking out of your life ever again."

She nodded, giving her brother another long hug before she followed Simon from the room, her hand tight in his as he led her after the nurse. She finally stood beside Blackie, watching as he tossed restlessly, picking at the covers and then trying to rise. Her hand came down on his, and he stilled, his hand flipping over to clutch at hers.

"Jewel? You're here? You're safe?" Blackie's eyelids flickered but didn't totally open.

"I am, Blackie. Now, you need to lie still. You've just had surgery."

"I have? No, that's not possible. I need to get up. I need to find Julia. She's not safe." He shoved at the blankets, staring at the IV line before he pulled it out and reached up and pulled the cardiac monitor leads from his chest, sending the machine into a wild beeping.

The nurses hit the room on a run, heading for Blackie. They tried to get him back into bed but he fought them, calling for Julia. Finally, Julia moved in front of them, her hands finding Blackie's face and she kissed him. He stopped, his eyes sliding closed, as his hands grasped her arms.

"Julia, it's you?" Eyes opened part way as he stared up at her. "You're here? They didn't get you?"

"No, Blackie. They haven't. Now, do what the nurses are asking you to do. We need you to lie back down. They have to put the IV back in and the leads back on you."

Blackie stared up at her, a frown in place, and shook his head. "No, I need to get out of here. I need to keep you safe." His eyes slid closed as his body sagged.

"No, what you need to do is to lie back down, okay? Here, put your head on your pillow. There, comfy? Tuck your feet in. The nurses have to do some stuff for you." Julia tried to extricate her hand from his grip but his only tightened. She looked up at the nurses, consternation on her face.

"It's okay, dear." The older nurse spoke, a gentle smile on her face. "He must really love you."

Julia shook her head, her eyes thoughtful. "I guess."

"What do you mean, you guess? I would say he does. How long have you two been going out?"

The nurses' glances held shock when Julia started to laugh. "Um, just a few days? Maybe a week?" She grinned, suddenly comfortable and safe in Blackie's love. "Do you believe in love at first sight?"

The nurses paused for a moment, exchanging glances, before the first one spoke. "I never did before, but I guess I do now. He's settled back down. Let's see if we can keep him that way. Don't leave his side, if you can help it. He'll be here for another hour or so and then we'll take him to a room." She paused to touch Julia's shoulder. "He'll be fine, dear. The wound wasn't as bad as it initially looked."

"Thank you." Julia looked around for a chair, finally perching on the side of the stretcher, her hand still tight in Blackie. "Will I be in the way here?"

The nurses started to laugh. "Not likely, seeing as he won't let go of you."

Chapter 11

$\mathscr{B}$lackie nodded to something his father asked, pain evident for a moment on his face, as he sat on the couch in the B&B living quarters. He had refused to stay in hospital any longer than a day, against everyone's wishes, but he saw the look Julia gave him and knew she understood. He had to find this fellow, Benny she called him, before he hurt Julia and he wasn't sure how to go about it.

Julia sat beside him, her hand on his for a moment, before she tucked the blanket around him. He reached to hug her close to him, pressing a kiss to her temple.

Simon paced in front of him, trying to make sense of what Blackie had finally told him. Samuel had gone through the office building as Julia had suggested and had legally obtained the material stored outside of Hal's office. He and Jacob were spreading the documents out on the coffee table even as Simon watched. There had to be something there.

"What was it you said again, Blackie? What did he actually say to you?" Jacob sat back on heels, his eyes on Blackie.

"I can't really remember, Jacob. He muttered it as I was going down. Something about getting Julia." He looked over at Julia, who had sat forward, her eyes on the paperwork. "Julia?"

Julia didn't hear him, her fingers sorting through the papers, before they stopped. She drew in a sharp breath. "There. That's what you need." She handed a paper to Simon before gathering all she had sifted through and putting them in order of date. She handed these to Jacob. "Now, you go through these and see if you recognize any names, events, etc. Simon, do you have that paperwork I gave you earlier? I need to go through it as well. I think we'll find we'll match dates and names."

Simon was to his car and back with his briefcase almost before she stopped speaking, opening it and handing her the sheaf of papers.

"Here, you go through it and then we'll match it with what Jacob and Josh are working on." He looked over at Blackie, whose head was back and his eyes closed. "I think we lost Blackie somewhere along the way, Julia."

She turned, her hands coming out to tuck the blanket tighter around him. "He shouldn't have left the hospital yet. But he was determined to. I couldn't say no when he begged me to help him leave."

"None of us could, Julia." Samuel stood watching the couple. "Now, what have you come up with?"

"This. These are all in chronological order. Jacob, have you found anything yet?"

He nodded. "I have. There are names that recur. I think he was running a protection racket and Timothy was right. But there's more than that." Jacob sat back, his eyes on Finn. "Finn, when we were looking back through all the information on the founding fathers, did we go back just to them or did we get back any further?"

"I think with yours we got back further, back to England or Ireland if I remember correctly. Why?"

"Because Hal seems to have connected with a gang from over there and brought people here to town. I can't determine who or if they are still here in town."

Samuel paused in his pacing, his eyes on Julia. "Julia? Did you know anything about this?"

She shook her head. "He was careful not to let me see who he was speaking with. That was guaranteed. Jonathan may know more than I do, but if I remember rightly, Hal changed how he did things after Jonathan left. He became much more secretive than before."

She turned to face Samuel. "How long has Jonathan been around?"

"For years, Julia. He had no idea what you were going through. Trust me. He would have gotten you out of there had he known. He has had someone watching out for you." He nodded at the paperwork she held. "Sort through that and then we'll compare the two piles." He turned and walked away, leaving her staring after him

She felt a hand on her arm and looked around. Blackie was watching her and then reached to draw her close to him, taking the papers from her hands.

"Dad's right, you know. Let it go, if you can. We can't change the past. God will provide us the wisdom and the resolution we need for you."

She nodded, her hair brushing against his chin. "I know that in my head. It's my heart that's having the trouble figuring it out." She reached and took the paperwork back, staring at it for a moment before she thrust it back into his hands and was up and out of the room, the men staring after her. Finn had been standing watching and followed her friend.

"Julia?" Finn tapped at the door to Julia's room. When invited, she cracked the door open, to find Julia standing in the centre of the room, her eyes on the picture above the bed.

"Finn? Where's that picture from?"

"The picture?" Finn shrugged. "I have no idea. We've had it for as long as I can remember. Why?"

Julia walked towards it. "Can I take if off the wall?"

"Sure. Why?" Finn moved to help.

Julia laid the picture of an old house and barn down on the bed before flipping it over. "Hal talked about a picture like this one time with Mom. He accused her of getting rid of it." She ran her fingers along the edge of the backing, before frowning. "There's something about this picture. I feel it, Finn. Would your mother object if we loosened the backing on it?"

Mary stood at the door. "No objection whatsoever, Julia. If it helps. Let me see, how is it fastened?"

"Staples, Mom. Just a moment." Finn was off the bed and back in a moment with a nail file. "Here. We can work this under the staples without damaging the backing."

Working carefully, Finn did just that, handing the staples to Julia. Mary stood, interest on her face. Finally pulling gently on the loosened backing, Finn moved it away and set it down, staring at what was there.

"Julia, how did you know?" Finn and Mary both stared at her.

"I have no idea. That picture has been bothering me all along. Now I know why. Who put those documents there? And what exactly are the?"

"Here, take them out, and then we'll go find the men. Maybe they'll have an idea of what we've found. Finn?" Mary realized she had lost Finn's attention.

"Julia, do you know what this is?" Finn looked up, her eyes on Julia.

Julia shook her head. "I have no idea about old papers. That's what you do."

Finn sat back down on the bed, carefully searching through the papers she had in her hands. "There are deeds here, a will, a court document, jail records. What did we find?"

"What are the names on them?" Julia sat beside her, leaning over to look. "Oh no! Those are Hal's parents. What did they do? Theses can't be legitimate documents. Well, maybe some of them, but not the deeds.

They can't pass the land or buildings on, can they?"

"It depends on where they're located." The three women looked up to see Timothy standing there.   He entered the room, reaching for the papers Finn handed him, flipping through them.   "From what I can see, they can't on these properties. They belong to the founding families. Now, this jail record. It's not for his father, Finn. It's for Hal himself, as a young man. Well, well, well! What do we have here?" He looked up, compassion on his face as he faced Julia.

Julia stared at him, not quite sure what his look meant. "Timothy? You're scaring me." She glanced behind him to see Blackie and Jacob standing there. She sighed. "I came up here to be alone.   That's not working so well.   Can we go back downstairs now and Timothy, you can explain what you mean?"

Timothy gave a light laugh, his eyes not showing his mirth as he shared a glance with Mary. "We can do that. Mary, you need to be putting out the tea items anyway. Finn, you can help. The rest of us are going to go through these and compare them to what we have already. I think we're finally getting somewhere. And Julia, dear, you will tell us how you knew about that painting."

❄ ❄ ❄ ❄ ❄ ❄

Blackie found Julia the next morning standing in the backyard, her arms wrapped around herself, her eyes on the sky. He came up and wrapping his own arms around her, drew her back against him.

"Jewel?"

She turned her head and looked up at him. "Just thinking, Blackie. Do you really think Hal had something to do with dad's death? I know Timothy does by the questions he has asked."

Blackie shrugged. "He's looking at any and all possibilities as is Dad. Come on." He tucked her tight to him and walked towards the storage barn at the back. "Mary was looking for something and she said you'd know where it was."

"And what was that?" She waited as he unlocked the door, reaching around him to turn on the lights. "Something for the kitchen?" When he didn't answer, she turned, finding his eyes on her, a slight smile curving his lips.

"You. She sent me after you." He reached and pulled her to him, his lips covering hers in a kiss before he hugged her tight. "She knew I just needed some time with you."

Julia pushed away. "We can't do this, Blackie. Not right now. Not while we're in danger."

He refused to let go of her hand, pulling her back to him. "We can. No one knows how long they have on earth. That's in God's hand." He watched as she mulled that over before he sighed. "I'm not rushing you, Jewel. Just think about it, okay?"

She finally nodded. "It is, Blackie. Just let me take my time. I've never had freedom before and I need to get through that before I jump into anything else."

"That's what God has been saying to me, Jewel. I won't rush you, but please, don't walk away from me." He realized he was begging and sighed, regretting his words as soon as he said them. "That wasn't fair. I shouldn't have said that."

She stood for a moment, staring at him. "Are you for real? You really just apologized to me. No one does that in real life." She turned to walk away, her footsteps slowing and then stopping as she heard his sigh and then his words.

"My family does, Jewel. It's how I was raised. If your words hurt someone, you make it right. That's life. Not everyone can do that. Sometimes the hurt goes too deep and words are said in hurt and anguish. I've seen it happen."

Blackie felt the blow that hit him, driving him to his knees and then to the floor, not seeing his assailant but hearing Julia's scream. His body hit where the wound was, pain flooding his body, darkening his vision. He didn't hear Julia's screams as she fought to get to him, restrained by men's hands, hands that clutched her arms and dragged her away from him. Blackie was hauled to his feet and dragged after her, not able to keep to his feet on his own. They were shoved through the back door and into the pastures that lined the back fence and then through the snow to a waiting vehicle. Shoved inside, Blackie's vision faded and he lost the fight to keep himself awake and alert.

Julia had fought her abductors, trying to get away, to reach Blackie. She had more bruises, she knew, and raised a hand to her face, to touch the soreness where she had been backhanded. Her eyes sought Blackie, wincing as he was manhandled and then shoved into the vehicle, sinking into stillness. She moved to go to him, but stopped as the weapon the one masked man was holding on Blackie turned to his temple. She sank back, fear coursing through every cell of her body. She wouldn't, couldn't help him, not right now. She blinked back tears of fright and then jumped as a blindfold was drawn over her face.

She listened intently, but couldn't hear any words from the men. She raged inside, knowing that no one would have known they were gone, not until they didn't show up for a meal or unless someone came looking for them. And who knew when that would be.

She laid her head back on the seat, knowing she had to relax and listen. Maybe she could figure out where she was by the sound, but she knew better. That only worked in books or movies, not in real life. One thing she knew for sure what that she would do everything to keep Blackie alive, even giving up her own life, and try to find a way for them to escape.

She felt the vehicle stop and she was dragged from it and shoved forward, stumbling as she tried to walk, fighting to keep her balance and losing, falling forward on her hands and knees, the impact jarring through her. She was hauled to her feet and the hand kept on her arm to draw her towards a building. She was shoved inside, this time just managing to keep her feet. She heard the sound of a body being dumped near her, then the slam of a door and the clicking of a padlock.

She waited, for what she wasn't sure, until she sank to her knees, feeling trapped once more. She could feel the panic rising inside her and struggled not to give in to the despair she felt. It was a losing battle and she curled forward, her arms wrapped around her head as the sobs came. This is not where I wanted to be. I thought You had given me my freedom, Lord, so what I am now a captive again? She sobbed until there were no tears left to fall but stayed curled up, not wanting to face anything or anyone. Who knew how long it would be before they were either free or dead? She had no doubt that was the plan, and she knew exactly who had arranged it.

Chapter 12

Finn was on a mission. Her mother said she had told Blackie where to find more of the Christmas cellophane she needed for her packages but he hadn't come back. Finn searched the storage shed and then the house, not finding either Blackie or Julia. She grew afraid.

She turned as she heard her name called and walked into Jacob's arms.

"Aren't you working, Jacob?"

"I was, but God told me I needed to be here. Why?"

She looked up at him and then around. "I can't find either Julia or Blackie. Mom sent him to the storage shed but he's not there. They're not in the house either. They wouldn't just walk away."

Jacob's arm swept around Finn and he rushed her into the house, his phone coming out as he called for reinforcements. Finn stared at him, fear on her face.

"Jacob? What do you think happened to them?" She didn't see Samuel appear in the doorway behind her, concern on his face.

"I don't know, Finn. Stay here. Samuel, come with me." Jacob ran for the storage shed, Samuel on his heels.

"Jacob?"

"Blackie and Julia have disappeared." He paused at the door to the shed, not entering, knowing that he couldn't, not until the police had been through it.

"No, not that!" Samuel looked around, stepping to the end of the building. "There. Tracks leading to the pasture at the back." He turned, his eyes fearful but determined. "Tell Simon that. Maybe they can track them, somehow."

Jacob had his phone out, speaking rapidly to Simon, who was on his way from Merryville.

"He'll be about twenty minutes. He's sending officers around to search. He wants us to stay away from the area and from the shed if we can."

"That we can do. Lord, please, bring them home."

Jacob watched with compassion as his friend's father stood, eyes raised to heaven in prayer before he spoke. "They're in God's hands, but that's little comfort, now isn't it?"

"We have to trust that, Jacob." Samuel turned, his keen eyes on the younger man. "What did you four discover with the paperwork?"

"I really don't know, Samuel. I had to go take a call from a client and never got back to the others. Blackie was working through it today, I think. He may have come up with something I don't know about."

"He'll have left notes, I know that." He turned as he heard men moving towards him. "Let's talk to the officers. Then we'll get out of their way so they can investigate and you and I will go look for Blackie's notes."

❄ ❄ ❄ ❄ ❄ ❄

Blackie stirred, his head going to his abdomen where pain shot through the wound. He felt it, not sure if it had opened up again. He groaned as he rolled to his back, his eyes opening to darkness and cold. He pulled himself to a sitting position, shrugging deeper into his jacket and pulling it tighter around him. Somehow, he needed to get to his feet and wasn't sure if he even could.

He felt a hand on his face and turned, barely seeing Julia's face in the dark. He could make out the track of the tears on her face, mingled with the dirt.

"Jewel?" His voice came out as a croak. "Are you okay?"

"Okay? That's relevant isn't it, considering we locked up in some building who knows where. And they hurt you again." She reached for his jacket, pulling down the zipper and pulling up his shirt and sweater. "There's no blood on your T-shirt. That's good. But it had to have hurt."

He shoved her hands aside and pulled his sweater and shirt back down, zipping up his jacket. "Help me up." He stared as she shook her head. "Help me up, Jewel, or I swear, I'll crawl over to a wall and drag myself up, probably tearing the incision open."

She sighed. "Blackie, please. You've just come back to me."

"Now, Julia." He met her eyes and nodded. "Please? I need to see what I can find out about where we are."

"I've searched. I didn't see anything we can use as a weapon or any way we can get out."

Blackie gave a quick grin. "You weren't in the armed forces, love. We learned all kinds of tricks. Now, please, help me. I already know it's going to hurt."

He stood for a moment, his arm around her shoulders, catching his breath against the pain. He knew it had only been a few days since the attack and he shouldn't have come home, not yet. But something had made him and now he knew why. God had prompted him to come, to be there for his Julia when she needed him.

"Do you have any idea where we are?"

"None. They blindfolded me. I think there were four? Two had you and two had me. Oh, and a driver." She paced, anger emanating from her. "It has to be Hal. Will he never leave me alone?"

"When I get my hands on him, he will." Blackie paced the building, his hands running over the walls and then the doors. He frowned as he found the windows and tried them.

"Jewel, did you see any sign of any cameras?"

She moved towards him. "No, I didn't but they could have hidden them."

He shook his head. "They wouldn't go to that extreme. I think we're out in the country somewhere, just where I have no idea." He shoved at the window, stopping to hold his side. "This one is loose. I need to get it up and then you can climb through. When you get out, find some shelter and run for it."

She shook her head. "Not without you."

"I'll be right behind you. I need to know you're safe, so please run."

She finally nodded, reaching to help him push at the window. Cold air rushed in, stinging their faces. Blackie's hands were on Julia's waist as she jumped for the window, her legs sliding through and then she was dropping to the ground, her eyes searching the blackness, see another building behind the one they were in. She ran for it, knowing that she had to. If Blackie didn't make it out, she had to get to help. She paused, her back to rough wood siding, her breath coming in pants. She started as she heard a sound, then relaxed as she felt Blackie's hand reaching for hers and pulling her away from the area and onto the road.

"We'll follow this for now. I don't think they'll be back before dawn." He glanced at the sky, knowing he would have to find them shelter somewhere. Those were snow clouds, he thought, shivering at the thought. He wasn't used to snow.

They slugged through the debris on the road, Blackie's eyes following the tire tracks before he lost sight of them as clouds covered the moon. He shivered, drawing his coat closer around him, praying they could find help soon. He stumbled, barely keeping his balance, as Julia gave a cry and reached for him, her arms around him the only thing holding him upright.

"Blackie, we need to rest. You can't go on." Her voice was desperate as she searched for a place for them to rest. She thought she recognized the area and with sinking heart, realized they were miles from the B&B, miles from Mistletoe, a town going on with its Christmas celebrations, not realizing the danger some of its inhabitants were facing. She knew tomorrow would be the annual parade through the down town, where the children would be welcomed into each business and given small gifts and treats and that the carollers would be making their rounds tomorrow night.

She finally saw what she was looking for, a small rutted laneway leading away from the road. She directed Blackie that way, staggering under his weight as he slumped for a moment, her arms feeling weighted as she held him upright.

"This way, Blackie. There's a cabin down here. I'm not sure if it's still occupied or not, but there will be shelter either way. Just hold on to me, please. Don't fall. I'd never get you on your feet again. Blackie!" The tears lacing her voice reached him and he nodded.

"I'll make it, love.   Head us in the right direction."

Julia stopped at the edge of the clearing, dismayed to see a dim light in the cabin and smoke rising from it.   She had prayed that it would be empty, but it wasn't. Now her prayer was that they were friends and would help her.   Blackie seemed oblivious to her concern, his only thought to stay upright and not fall, taking Julia with him. That he couldn't do.

Julia tapped at the door, waiting with apprehension as she heard shuffling coming towards the door and then the door cracking open. She sighed. She knew the man there. Old Jack, she thought. What was he doing out this far?

"Julia?"   Jack pulled the door open and then reached to take part of her burden. "What are you doing out here? Who's this with you?"

"It's Blackie. I think you've met him, haven't you?"

Jack stopped, staring at Blackie. He knew of him. "He's that medic fellow, ain't he?"

"He is, Jack. I need your help. He was stabbed two or three days ago and today we were kidnapped. We were left way up the road. I need to get him laying down so I can check his wound."

Jack nodded, even as he helped Julia walk Blackie over to the second bunk in the cabin. Blackie sank to the bed, his head bobbing forward before Julia gently forced his shoulders to the bed and then helped Jack lift his feet up to rest there as well. She tore open his jacket, her hands frantic to find his wound.

"Oh, no! Jack, he's bleeding. I can't tell if he's broken open any stitches or not."

"Go, grab the lamp, Julia. Let me take a look." Jack's gruff voice had changed and strengthened, as if looking after Blackie had given him a purpose. He set the boots he had removed neatly under the end of the bunk and reaching, pulled a small table over close.

"Set the lamp here, girl, and then go get me some hot water. The kettle had just boiled. There's a clean basin by the sink, and you'll find towels in the second drawer."

He peered around at her, his light gray eyes troubled. "Go. Do what I've asked."

She finally nodded, flying to do what he asked, and finding the first aid kit where he called to her to find. She flew back to his side, her hand to her mouth as she watched him pull the bloodied T-shirt back.

"You ain't going to faint on me, are you, girl? Cause if you are, go sit down somewheres. I can only look after one of you at a time."

"I'll be fine, Jack. Just let me help." She handed him the cloths and then the bandages as he called for them.

"There, that should do it. Thank you, girl." Jack stood, heading for the small kitchen to wash up and get rid of the debris. "I ain't seeing that he ripped open more than one or two stitches. I think what I did will help." He turned, his eyes suddenly hardening. "Who did this to you, girl?"

She shook her head. "I have no idea, Jack, but I think it was Hal's friends."

"That no-good Hal? Up to his tricks again, is he?"

She could hear Jack muttering under his breath and went towards him. "Jack? What do you know about Hal?"

"More than most people. He's the reason I lost my home. He stole it from me, just like he stole from others." He peered at her. "I know your mom is married to him, but she knew what she was doing and walked into it with open eyes. Your father wasn't so lucky."

"Jack? Whatever do you mean?"

"You never knew?" He watched her keenly, seeing the distress in her face and the questions. He sighed. He didn't want to be the one to tell her but it looks as if it was his story to tell. Thanks a lot, Lord, he muttered. I'm not the one to be doing this, but for some reason, You seem to think so. You'll have to give me the words. You know I ain't much of a one for talking.

"Sit, girl. Here. I only have tea. Hope that suits." He slid a tin mug in front of her, his eyes rising to check on Blackie.

"Anything hot works today, Jack." She wrapped her hands around the mug, relishing the warmth, her eyes on the liquid in it. "What was you need to tell me? Please? I need to know and it doesn't look as if anyone else is able to tell me."

Jack sat, his own tin mug in front on him as he rubbed at the back of his neck. Where did he start, he wondered? No matter what he said, she'd be hurt, and he decided she'd been hurt enough. He sighed, finally ready to tell the story that he had kept in his heart for so many years, a story he knew would hurt those around him and that he didn't want but couldn't help.

"Jack?" A soft hand closed around his, bringing his eyes to it and then to her face. It had been years since he had felt a female hand on his. They usually ran away from him, and he couldn't say that he blamed them.

"Julia, what I am about to say goes back many years, years you'll never get back with your daddy. I wish I could have stopped it, but I couldn't. I didn't have proof until now of what actually happened."

Julia stared at him, wonder on her face, not sure what he meant but knowing I her heart that his word would change her life dramatically, not necessarily for the good.

She prayed for them all, her heart raised in a
petition like she had never done before.

Chapter 13

Samuel turned as he heard steps behind him and Simon, Josh and Jacob approached him. He looked back down at the paperwork he had spread out on the dining room table, sorting it out by date and event.

"Samuel, where do we stand with what you have there?" Simon stood for a moment, his eyes on his friend, and then on the paperwork.

"It's a mess, that's what, Simon. How did he get away with what he did for all these years? You won't believe all I'm finding. I don't believe it myself." He stared at the paper he had in his hand, a list of deeds Hal had been guilty of. "Assault. Robbery. Blackmail. Extortion." He shot a look behind the men. "Jonathan's not here?"

Josh shook his head. "No. Were you expecting him?"

"I was praying that he wasn't." He handed Josh a paper he had picked up as he spoke, watching keenly as he read it and paled, before passing it to Jacob and from Jacob to Simon.

Simon's hand stilled as he read before he raised his head. "This changes everything, now doesn't it? I'll get someone on this. I'm too close, I know my lieutenant will want someone else to investigate this."

"Talk to Paul in my office. I've had him working on this. He may have some information for you that will help." He sighed, his hand rubbing the back of his neck. "I don't like this, not with Levi and Julia missing. Hal must have them."

Julia watched as Jack rose and paced over to the bunk, checking on Blackie and as she suspected, gathering his thoughts. He stood for a moment, his eyes on the younger man's face, knowing Julia had found the one God had planned for her. She was fortunate. He had thought he had all those years ago but lies and deceit had driven her away, not on his part. He had motive for revenge but chose not to go that route.

He sat once more at the table, sipping at his tea for a moment before he finally spoke.

"You'll need to let me say it in all one go, Julia. If you stop me, I just can't continue. It's been building in me for far too many years. Can you do that for me?"

She nodded. "I can, but it will be hard. Jack?"

He watched her face before he finally nodded. "All right then. I have no idea where to start."

"The beginning is usually a good place to start, isn't it?"

He shook his head at her levity, then began to speak.

"Years ago, I loved someone dearly. We had planned to marry but someone went to her, telling her lies about me, that I was dishonest, that I stole and assaulted people. No matter how much I protested my innocence, she walked away, taking part of my heart with her. She left town and I lost contact with her.

"The person who did this was Hal. Even as a teenager and young man, he was thoroughly dishonest. But he hid it so no one could prove anything, no matter their suspicions. I couldn't prove he's the one who said what he did, she refused to talk about it. Hal has continued as he was, getting worse and worse.

"He is not one of the descendants of the founding families, thank God for that. I'm not sure how long his family has been in town but I think his father was the one to move here. There were rumours about what he was mixed up in." He paused to sip at his tea.

"Now, about you. You have no idea how glad I am that you got away from Hal. He would eventually have killed you, and will continue to try unless we put him away. Unfortunately, your mother doesn't or won't see what he's doing. That I can't figure out.

"Your daddy was a wonderful man, caring, compassionate, loving. He loved you and your brother so much." He paused for a moment, as if to say something, then shook his head.

"I don't know if you know the real way your father died. It wasn't a sudden death as you've been told or how it was spread around town. Your father was held hostage and starved, finally having a heart attack. Your mom tried to put out that it was a car accident. He was found in a wrecked car but that's not how he died. He was way too young to have died. And it was Hal who did this to him. He caused your daddy's death."

Julia stared at him, horror and shock on her face, her hands over her mouth, before she began to shake.

"It was, Julia. I just now have the evidence I need to take to that Simon fellow and have him track down Hal and his cronies. But you're not safe until we find him."

"But if we're not safe, where do we go, Jack? I can't bring any more danger to Finn and her family."

"No, you can't. I have a place you two can hide out in. No one knows about it. It's not this place but it's not far. If I can get your fellow there early this morning, the snow will wipe out the tracks and they won't find you. I have a way of keeping in touch with you."

She finally nodded, rising and walking over to Blackie, slipping to her knees, an arm under his neck to raise his head to sip at the glass of water. She watched him as she stood for a moment before turning back to Jack and sitting near him.

"There's more to your story, isn't there, Jack?" She tilted her head to watch him, frowning at familiar movements of the head and hands.

"There is, Julia, and I'm not sure if I should even tell you."

"You're related to Dad, aren't you?"

He finally nodded, his hands reaching out to cover hers. "People in town have forgotten. Jack's not my real name. It's a name I chose to use when I came back here." He paused, his eyes taking on a faraway look. "Your daddy was my brother. I was away, overseas when he died and couldn't get home to the funeral. Your mom made sure I didn't find out for long afterwards."

Julia stared at him, her mouth suddenly widening into a huge smile.

"Uncle Ben. It's you. No wonder I always felt a connection with you."

He held up a finger. "You can't tell anyone, girl. It would mean both of our deaths, if you do. You can't even tell your fellow over there until Hal and his cronies are behind bars. It's too dangerous."

She nodded even as she rose to hug her uncle. "I've missed you. I had almost forgotten about you. Mom made sure of that."

She sat beside him, her hands clutching him. "Why, Jack? Oh, I should call you Uncle Ben!"

"Not yet, girl. We need to keep that between us, at least for now. Don't even tell your fellow over there. He doesn't know Hal like I do. He'll use that against you and against him."

She nodded. "I know he will. I won't let him. He's taken enough of my life."

They talked for a long while before she sighed, then rose, walking over to drop on the floor by Blackie, her arm crossing his chest as she laid her head beside him, her heart praying as she had never prayed before. Her eyes closed and she slept.

Jack watched her for a while before he rose and gathered her up, placing her on his bunk and covering her up. He had watched from afar as she had grown. His heart broke to know the abuse she had told him about, that he hadn't had the evidence he needed before to prevent this. He drew up the blanket, tucking it around her, just like he used to when she was a toddler and he had gotten to watch her. He thought of Jonathan and knew he was in town but that he had to avoid him. Jonathan would know who he was. He was that keen, that young fellow, he thought.

He walked over to check on Blackie, finding the bleeding had slowed. He was worried that Blackie would develop an infection and he didn't have what he needed to give him. He couldn't even get what he needed from the forests at this time of year, and he didn't want to walk away from these two to go get the medications. He knew the physician in town, that he would gladly give him the antibiotics and treatments he needed. For you see, Jack too had been a medic in the navy, and Allan knew this. He trusted Jack in a way few had. Allan also knew exactly who he was and helped him in ways most people wouldn't.

Blackie stirred in the early morning, finding hands helping him sit up and drink. He nodded at a question and then slipped back into unconsciousness, pain evident on his face as he did so. Jack stood over him, fear warring with concern. He turned to look at Julia, knowing he had to get her up and get them moved.

Julia stirred as she heard Jack's voice and nodded, even as she sat up, her eyes flying to Blackie.

"How is he, Jack?" She pleaded with him to say he was better.

"He's hurting, girl, and I have to hurt him even more to move him. Come on. Let's get you two out of here."

"But how? We don't have a vehicle."

Jack smirked at her. "I do. It's a little ramshackle but it runs real smooth. Let's get your fellow out the back door."

Jack lifted Blackie in his arms, grunting a bit at his weight, then nodded for Julia to open the door leading from the kitchen. She stood, open mouthed, staring at the old truck there.

"This is yours? I've seen it around town and never knew."

"Not too many people do. That's a blessing right now. I don't think Hal or his cronies know. Here, you climb in the middle and hold on to your fellow real tight."

Julia's arms surrounded Blackie as Jack pulled away from the cabin, heading back to Mistletoe and then through the quiet early morning streets. He chose a street near the edge of town, heading for the quarry and then beyond, finally pulling in beside a small house and parking behind it. He ran around the truck and once more gathered Blackie into his arms, handing Julia the keys.

"It's all ready to use. There's a bedroom just off the kitchen. We'll put him there. It's the easier spot to look after him."

Jack stood back, his eyes assessing Blackie and knowing he had to go for help. Blackie was starting to run a fever and he couldn't treat it without supplies. His hand on her arm drew Julia back to the kitchen.

"The kitchen well stocked with canned and dry goods. Keep him warm and get as much water down him as you can. Broth if possible. There are some cans of that here." He looked at her, concern on his face. "Are you able to do that for me?"

She nodded, her eyes fearful, but determination on her face. "I can. But I need you to do something for me. You need to find Simon and Samuel, Blackie's father. You need to tell them what you know and today. I don't think we'll have much longer."

"No, we don't. Hal's been released, I hear, and is on the hunt for you two. You should be safe here. No one knows about this place. It's not in my name and the name it is in no one knows."

"Jack?"

He shook his head as he reached for his keys and then the door handle. "No, I won't say. Just take care of your fellow. I'll be back as soon as I can." He paused. "Your father was a real Christian, and Lord knows I've tried to live that way. Pray like you never have before, Julia. I know you believe." He was gone before she could respond.

Jack watched as Simon walked back to his vehicle. He suspected he had been in the B&B all night. He approached carefully, eyes watchful in the dim morning light, before he paused beside Simon.

"Simon, you and I need to talk and talk now. Where can we meet? I don't want to be seen talking with you."

Simon's fingers continued to turn the key in his vehicle lock as he listened. "You sound like you could use a good meal, my friend. I hear tell the back door of The House is unlocked at this time of the morning. Josh will feed you."

Jack shuffled off, back into the character he had lived for so many years. Simon slid into his car, his eyes watchful, before he drove a circuitous route to Josh's cafe, parking down the street, and making his way quickly to the back door. Josh looked up from his prep table and nodded towards his office. Simon raised a hand in greeting, then snagged some muffins and tea. He knew that was Jack's preference.

He set the food down on the table by Jack, shrugging out of his jacket and turning to hang it on the coat rack before he sat himself, picking up his cup of coffee and inhaling the aroma. He waited as Jack ate, knowing Jack well enough to know that he would speak when he was ready to. He needed a break and a break soon. He feared for Blackie's life and that of his lady, Julia. He had no idea where they were.

"They're alive, Simon." He almost missed Jack's low voice and spun in his chair to stare at him. Jack's keen eyes peered at him, eyes Simon suddenly realized were clear and calm, not what he had been led to expect from him.

"What did you just say?" Simon kept his own voice low.

"They're alive, Simon. I have them tucked away somewhere safe. We need to keep them there for as long as we can." He took another bite of muffin, his eyes on it. "Does Josh bake these himself? They're good."

"Yes, he does, and yes, they are." Simon breathed out a sigh of frustration. "Explain yourself, Jack."

Jack reached for a napkin and wiped his fingers, then sipped at his tea. "I said I have them tucked away. Somehow they escaped from where they were locked up. Julia helped get Blackie to me and we've dressed his wound. It was broken open again." He tilted his mug towards Simon. "She's a wonder and good for him. Doc will get me some supplies and I'll dress it again when I see them."

"No, when we see them."

"Not happening, Simon. If you go with me, Hal or his people will see you and follow us. He's watching each one of you now, including Blackie's father and also the B&B. There is no way to get you to them without being seen."

Simon sat back, frustrated, knowing the truth in Jack's words. "I guess. But what did they tell you?"

"Blackie's been out of it for most of the night. Julia finally slept until I woke her early this morning to move them. No one should be able to find the house where I have them. And no, I'm not saying where. I trust you men, but who's to say someone hasn't bugged this office or anywhere you gather."

Simon nodded, looking around as he heard Josh saying something outside the door before he cracked it open and slipped in.

"Simon, I don't have long before the breakfast rush starts and I'll likely be called out. What's the word?" Josh watched Jack closely, knowing something was different about him.

"Jack has them tucked away. Blackie's wound opened and Julia's fine. He won't say where though." Simon was not happy about that.

"Makes perfect sense to me. We need to keep them safe and we can't tell what we don't know." Josh studied Jack closer and realized who he looked like. Jack was watching him and nodded, a finger coming to his lips. "Jack, what can we get you to help out?"

"Doc's getting me supplies. I have food stashed there. Just need some fresh stuff and some bread. That will keep us for now."

"You're heading back there? Ask Amy in the kitchen for what you want. It's on the house. Tell her that."

Josh's question had him shaking his head. "Not until this afternoon when it gets dark. If I feel a real need I'll head back." He dug into his pocket, pulling out the papers he had prepared the night before and handing them to Simon. "Here. This is what you can do. I know for a fact that Julia's father was tortured and killed, why I'm still working on. Hal was behind it." He tapped the papers Simon held with a long forefinger. "Work through that, son. I think you'll find the evidence you need to finally put him away." Jack stood, his eyes shifting between the two men before he shook his head and slipped out the door.

Josh stared after him, then back at Simon, who was leafing through the papers, horror growing as he realized the implications of what Jack had just handed him.

"Simon?"

Josh's voice brought his head up and he shook it. "This is worse that I ever imagined. Jack, there, he found evidence that Hal had Julia's father killed, because he wanted what he had in property. I don't think it would have been a very pretty picture when he found out he got none of it."

Josh's shocked look stopped him. "Murder? That's what he's saying?" Josh's hand ran through his hair, before he rose and paced. "That just changes everything." He spun. "You'll need to talk to Samuel. Their lives are in more danger than we ever thought."

"I know. I just wish I knew where Jack had them stashed."

"He won't tell, I can guarantee you that." Josh rose. "Keep me in the loop and if I need to I'll cut myself free from here." He paused. "I don't like this, Simon. We need to make this a matter of prayer and strong prayer at that."

"We do and we have. Mary said the prayer chain had set up in the church prayer room, opening it up 24/7 until these two are home."

"That's good." Josh paused, not sure if he should admit he knew who Jack was relate to, but knew Jack has his reasons for not saying.

❋ ❋ ❋ ❋ ❋ ❋

Julia stood for a moment in the late afternoon, her eyes on the door, wondering when Jack would come back. Blackie's fever had worsened and he was fighting her when he roused, wanting to get up and go and find her, to protect her. She had only just been able to keep him still, but she knew eventually the fever would drive him to his feet and out the door, and she would be unable to stop him. She prayed as she hadn't prayed in years, fearing the worse and hoping for the best.

She paused in her walk as she heard footsteps and then voices. Her eyes flew to the door. Yes, all the locks were engaged, and she had kept the drapes and blinds closed, a suggestion of Jack's she was now glad he had made. Her hand at her throat, she crept towards Blackie's room, praying that whoever it was would leave.

187

She listened to the voices, two men, she thought, discussing the house and whether someone was in there. The doors were tried but didn't open. The doors shook as they were tried harder. Her head dropped in fear as she silently slipped into Blackie's room and shut the door, looking for anything to defend herself and finding nothing. Finally, she heard the voices moving away.

Jack, don't come back just yet. Not until they're gone. She turned towards the door, opening it once more and sneaking through the house to the front, where she peeked through the window on the front door. She didn't see anyone. She lowered herself back to the floor and leant against the wall. She couldn't take much of this, she thought, but then the determination not to let Hal win coursed through her. He was after a treasure that wasn't his. She wouldn't let that happen. She had never heard how the actual wills from the founding fathers worked, that only the founding families' descendants got what was in them. Even if she had, it was doubtful it would have eased her worry.

Hours later, dark had descended. She was careful to keep a light low, hoping if anyone saw it, they would think it was just a light on a timer. She heard quiet footsteps outside and grabbed up the fireplace poker she had found and kept near her. The locks opened and Jack stepped in, his eyes on the deck for a moment before he turned and saw Julia standing there, poker raised.

"Had some visitors, did you, girl?" Jack grinned as she shook the poker playfully at him.

"We did. I was so scared they would get in."

"Did they see you?"

She shook her head. "No, I had everything shuttered like you asked and then hid in Blackie's room. I recognized one of the voices. It was Tad, Hal's brother."

Jack nodded. "They're searching for you two, and it makes sense they would search every outlying building." He set his parcels on the table and shrugged out of his jacket, hanging in on a chair back. He nodded towards the bedroom. "How is he?"

"His fever has gone up. I've given him what I can, but it's a fight to keep him there. He keeps wanting to get up and find me." She sighed. "That's what he was like in the hospital that day. He kept forgetting I was there."

Jack grinned at her again. "That boy in there is in love with you, girl. That's as plain as the nose on your face." He watched with compassion as she nodded. "Now, let me have a look at him and dress his wound." He sorted through the parcels, finding the one that he wanted. "Doc sent out some medications and more dressings for me."

He paused at the doorway, his eyes on his niece as she moved to put away the food he had brought, his heart breaking for her. This was not how he had wanted to introduce himself to her again, but it seemed that was how God had it planned. He shook his head, not understanding the workings of the Lord, and headed into the bedroom.

He drew in a breath as he saw the wound, knowing they had a fight on their hands. It was no wonder he had a high fever. He hurried back to the kitchen, searching for a bowl and filling it with hot water, his words quiet and calm as he talked with Julia. She followed him, knowing what he had found. She had seen it earlier herself but hadn't touched it, not wanting to make it worse.

Blackie flinched and groaned, his body twisting as he fought the pain of the wound being cleaned. He finally laid still, Julia's hand on his cheek, her other hand holding his. They had gotten pain medication and antibiotics down him, but not without a fight. Jack watched the IV drip, adjusting it as necessary, giving Julia instructions on what to do if he wasn't around. In his heart, he knew he wouldn't leave, not unless he absolutely had to. And the only way that would be was if Allan reached out to him by phone. He was the only one who had Jack's number.

Julia finally sagged down into a chair, her arms folded on the table, her head on her arms. Her uncle rested his hand on her back for a moment before he moved to the stove, coming back with the tea she needed. A quiet thank you, muffled by her arms, was all he got.

"Julia. Look up, please." Jack waited until she did, seeing the fatigue in the whiteness of her face and the dark circles under her eyes. "I talked to Simon and that

Josh. Simon has everything I know and he'll look into it." He grinned briefly. "He was a little put out that I wouldn't bring him out here."

"It's better that they don't come. It was too close a call today, Jack. If they had got in, I couldn't have stopped them."

"No, you couldn't have. That worries me." Jack sipped at his tea, eyes thoughtful as he worked through what had to be done. "Pray that what we've done for your fellow works. Because if he isn't better by morning, I'll have to take him to Doc, and they'll find us for sure. They'll be watching him too, and likely have someone at the hospital in Merryville."

She nodded. "I know that." She rose, dropping a kiss on her uncle's cheek. "Now that you're here, I'm going to get some sleep. Wake me in a couple of hours, will you?"

Jack didn't respond, knowing full well he wouldn't be doing that. He sighed, taking their cups to the sink and rinsing them out, setting them upside down on the drainboard, before he turned, crossing his arms over his chest, deep in thought. A

groan from Blackie had him heading that
way, concern wafting through him.

*B*lackie roused towards morning, his mouth dry and feeling like it was full of cotton balls. He felt the hand under his head, holding it up so he could sip, water he thought, but he wasn't even really sure of that. He groaned as his head was lowered, his hand going to his abdomen.

"Blackie, boy. Are you awake?" A rough voice reached him, kindness in it.

"No, not really. Why? Do I need to be? What day is it, any way? I need to find Julia. She's in danger." Blackie's eyes flickered opened and then closed, he was just too tired to keep them open.

"I need to look at your wound. It may hurt."

Blackie nodded, steeling himself for what he knew would come. He gritted his teeth, then relaxed, drifting off to sleep again.

Jack tucked the blanket up around Blackie's neck, feeling his forehead, glad to feel the coolness there. Blackie's fever had broken, but Jack knew only too well it could go up again. He was not out of the woods, yet, he thought. He reached to check the IV drip and then sat back down in the rocking chair he had placed near the bed, a light kept low the only illumination in the room, and reached for his Bible. He had just turned to a favourite passage when Blackie had roused, a passage about touching the hem of the Master's garment. It was a passage he had claimed many times over.

He turned as he heard soft footsteps as the dawn light cracked the morning sky. Julia stood in the door way, her hair still tousled, wearing what he suspected was a sweatshirt of Blackie's over her jeans. He had slipped unnoticed in the B&B and found Blackie's room the day before, carefully taking only a few clothes that he didn't think would be missed.

"Jack?" There was both dread and hope in her voice.

"He was awake, girl. The fever's broken for now, but we're not out of the woods yet. I'll have to go back to town to scout out the area again, but I won't leave for now. Maybe tomorrow."

"Tomorrow? Do we have until then?"

Jack nodded. "I suspect we do. We'll make sure we do." He rose and stopped beside her in the doorway. "He'll make it, Julia. Trust God on that."

She nodded, her eyes on Blackie. "I pray he does. He's been talking to me about treasures that we need to find. He tells me I'm his treasure. I don't see that, Jack. I'm broken, that's what I am."

Jack turned her to face him, sorrow filling him at her words, then anger at how she had been treated. "No, you are a treasure, Julia. God sees that in you. He is your treasure, first and foremost. Seek Him, and you'll find Him." Then he pointed at Blackie. "Next, that young man is there is a treasure God prepared for you. Don't chase him away." He paused, not quite sure how to continue. "Pearls are just grains of sand until the oyster coats them, making a gem that people pay a lot for. That happens with a lot of precious gems. Hardship and beatings and what have you make them what they become.   Don't let anyone put you down.""

She finally nodded.   "Thank you.   I forgot to ask. Has Simon found them yet?"

Jack turned her towards the kitchen, seating her and then reaching to fill the kettle, setting it back on the stove and turning on the burner, watching it for a moment as he thought. He finally shook his head. "No, he hasn't. He's getting close, but there's still a lot he has to work through. Hal is staying one step ahead of him, and I need to find out why."

Julia shook with fear at the thought of what lay ahead of them, her mind blanking out, not hearing the concern in Jack's voice as he called to her. A groan from Blackie reached through the darkness, bringing her to her feet and into his room, her hand on his head, finding it warm again

"Jack? His fever's back. What do we do now?"

"We fight it, girl, with everything we have. We'll keep him alive for you."

Chapter 14

Samuel stood in Josh's office, his eyes on the younger man.

"Who did you say was here?"

"An old fellow from around town. He does odd jobs for people to earn an income. He says he has Blackie and Julia stashed somewhere but won't tell us."

"I want to talk with him. Now, if posible."

Josh shook his head. "He's not in town. I've looked, knowing you would. I have no idea where he goes when he leaves town. No one does. He just comes and goes." Josh sank into his desk chair, rubbing a hand down his face. "He says they're safe. He also says Hal has people watching each one of us, the B&B and also Doc."

Samuel paced in the small area that was clear. "He would. I have documentation back that I need to go over with all of you. I guess it will have to be you, Jacob and Simon for now. I'll have to pretend to be Levi, I guess."

Josh started to laugh at that, bringing a welcome grin to Samuel's face. "I don't know about that, Samuel. Looking at you is like looking at Blackie in a few years."

Samuel just shook his head at Josh's jesting. "Are the other two heading this way or do we go theirs?"

"Here, I think. They're planning on showing up after I close. Simon has some things as well, he said." He turned as he heard the men's voices, Simon teasing Jacob about something, Jacob's voice raised in protest.

Simon stuck his head in the door. "Your staff are gone, Josh, but Amy said she left our meals in the warming oven. Let's go eat. I didn't have lunch and I'm starved."

Josh shook his head at him. "You're always hungry." He shoved himself upright, groaning to himself. It had been a long day, with two staff off sick, and tomorrow promised to be just as long.

They settled around the counter in the kitchen, Samuel's keen eyes watching his son's friends as they joked and teased one another. He knew they were deliberately doing this, to hide their worry from him. He finally pushed his plate away, wiping his mouth on his napkin, catching Simon's eyes as he did so.

"Samuel? You found something?"

"I have. David in my office did a real good in-depth search, finding information that we didn't know about." He paused, gathering his thoughts, and then reaching for his jacket to pull out the papers he had stuffed in there. "Now, let me think for a moment.

"Okay, so this is what he's found. Hal is not related to any of the founding families. That we knew. Nor is Julia's mother. Where she is from is not relevant at the moment but may become so. Julia's father was related to Finn's family, a cousin I think Timothy said. That we have confirmed. Because he is deceased, whatever he left goes to Julia and Jonathan. That has been what Hal has been after.

"David did find an interesting wrinkle. Julia's father, John, had a brother, Benjamin, who disappeared a number of years ago. He was in the service, came home after he found out John had died, returned to the service, mustered out and then disappeared. David wasn't able to access any further information on him because it suddenly became classified and unavailable. We haven't been able to find out why."

Simon nodded. "Do we have any idea where he ended up?" He turned as a sound from Josh. "Josh?"

Josh sighed, knowing he would have to tell what he knew. "I know where he is, but he really doesn't want it told about."

"And just how do you know that?" Jacob stared at him. "You can't leave us hanging like this, you know."

Josh nodded. "I can tell you, but we can't let anyone know we know." He groaned as they laughed at his choice of words. "Not quite how I meant to say that." He paused, his eyes on Samuel, knowing Samuel would really want to talk to the man. "It's Old Jack. He confirmed it this morning when we were meeting."

A flurry of talk broke out at that before Simon turned to Josh. "But he never said a word. Not that I heard."

"No, he didn't. He caught me watching him and realized I had figured out who he looked like. Julia and Jonathan do look like him."

Samuel nodded. "I've seen him around, just didn't realize he was so involved in this." He sighed. "He won't let us near him, I know that now. He'll look after Blackie and Julia."

Simon nodded as Jacob and Josh agreed. "That helps to make sense of what I found then. I knew there was someone in town watching them, but I didn't know who exactly. We've been digging into Hal's background. There is an officer on the way in from a town four hours away, with an arrest warrant for murder. Hal has been charged in a man's murder from there. That will take him out of here but that doesn't solve the problem of his friends watching for Blackie and Julia."

"We'll find them, Simon, and bring them to you. I have some of my men coming in this weekend. They're bringing the family back. They've wanted to be here, but I talked them into waiting."

Blackie's head turned restlessly as his eyes opened and stayed open. It was early the next morning. His body ached and he didn't know why. He felt for his ribs, finding the bandage just below them, but not knowing why he had it. He felt a cool hand feel his head and he looked up, a frown on his face. He didn't know the man.

"You're finally away, Blackie. That's good. Here. Take a sip of water." Jack raised Blackie's head to help him sip and gently lowered it once he was through.

"You've been through a lot, young man. There's a lady out there real worried about you. Here. Let's get you cleaned up some and then I'll go get her."

Julia looked up from the chair she had been sleeping in, not willing to head for her bed as she heard Jack's footsteps heading her way.

"Julia, girl. He's awake. At least he was. Come, see your fellow."

Julia scrambled from the chair, her feet tangling in the blankets, fighting until she was free, Jack holding her arm to help her stay upright.

"Did he speak, Jack?"

Jack shook his head. "Not yet." He watched with a small smile as she headed for Blackie.

She paused in the doorway, her eyes on Blackie, watching for him to rouse again. She walked quietly across the room, sitting on the side of the bed, causing his head to turn towards her and his eyes open.

"Julia? You're okay?" His voice was rough and not above a whisper.

"I am. I can't say the same for you, though. You scared me."

He reached for her hand, squeezing hers gently. "I'm sorry. I didn't mean to." He looked around. "Where are we?"

"Jack's place. He brought us here to keep us safe. We've been here for a couple of days. You won't remember that though. You've been pretty much out of it."

Blackie nodded, his eyes sliding closed, before he asked. "You'll stay, Julia? You won't disappear on me, will you, love?"

"No, Blackie. I won't. Not for the rest of our lives, if I can help it." She knew he didn't hear that, he was already asleep.

Jack stood in the doorway, his eyes watchful, a sad smile on his face. Her father should be here for this, he thought. But then if he was, maybe these two would never had met.

❄ ❄ ❄ ❄ ❄

"Jack, when do you head back into town?" Julia's question caught him off guard later that morning.

"Likely mid afternoon, seeing as your fellow is now sleeping. Why?"

She shrugged. "I just wondered. I want to know what's going on. Can you find one of the fellows and ask them?"

Jack gave a soft laugh. "Oh, I guarantee you I'll find them. They'll be on the look out for me."

She shook her head at him. "Just come back with some news." She turned back to the broth she was heating, not seeing the speculative look on his face.

Jack tapped at Josh's office door later, bringing Josh's head up and then entering, closing the door behind him.

"He's alive, Josh, before you ask. It was a struggle, but he's pulled through."

Josh was relieved to hear that, pointing at the chair for Jack to sit. "And Julia?"

"She's tired, worn out from nursing her fellow." He studied the younger man. "Where does the investigation stand?" His voice had lost the croak that Josh associated with him.

"Simon's arrested Hal for a murder in another town. The officer headed off with him around noon. His friends are still in town, but laying low right at the moment." Josh looked down at his desk, not seeing the paperwork he had been immersed in. "When will you bring them back into town?"

"Blackie needs two or three days to get some strength back. He's not got much left to fight with right now." Jack stood and stretched. "Did Simon take a look at the paperwork I left?

"He did. He's following up on a few leads. You had some interesting facts there for him. Facts that Blackie's father has confirmed."

Jack nodded. "I know Hal had Julia's father killed. I still have to prove that."

"And we will. With Hal gone, his friends may talk now. He'll be put away for a long while. The judge there said there would be no bail set, given his past history and what he is up to right now."

"That's good news, but he can still control his friends' movements from there."

"Not if we can help it, and we're trying our best to make sure that he can't."

Josh stood for a moment, watching the door swing closed behind Jack as he walked away. He sighed, knowing he would not be finishing his paperwork now. He had to find Samuel. He turned, hearing a noise behind him but not seeing the man who struck the blow, knocking him into his chair, slamming his head on the desk and sending him to the floor unconscious. The man stood over him for a moment, cursing at the turn of events. He needed Josh to talk and know he wouldn't be able to. He followed Jack, unaware that Jack knew he was there and had stopped to ask someone to go back and check on Josh.

Jack finally ducked into a doorway, listening to the footsteps and watching as the man passed him, darting out and taking him down. Twisting his arm up behind him, he yanked him to his feet and shoved him back towards The House, finding Simon running his way.

"You caught him! Great!" Simon slid to a halt, his balance off for a moment as he hit a patch of ice. "He's knocked Josh out, but Jacob's with him. Let's get him to the department." He peered closer at the man. "Well, well, well! Just who did you catch, Jack?"

"Hal's brother and his partner in crime." Jack shoved the man forward, his voice quiet as he talked to Simon.

Josh looked up, pain in his eyes, as Jack walked back through his door.

"We caught the man, Josh.   Hal's brother."

Josh went to nod, then decided against doing just that. "Good! Now how many more do we need to find?"

Jack grinned for a moment, then sobered. "I think you'll need to find five or six. That should do it. Also Julia's mother. She's not innocent in any of this."

"No, she's not. Simon's looking for her but she's disappeared."

Jack nodded.   "Thought she would. She has family back in her home town. They'll hide her."

Josh stared at him for a moment. "You seem to know her well."

Jack sighed. "I do, unfortunately." He paced again.   "I need to get Blackie and Julia back, but it will be a couple of days."

"Whenever. Just keep them safe."

Chapter 15

$\mathcal{B}$lackie stood for a moment, his hands braced against the door frame, his eyes closing as he caught his breath. It was two days after he had finally woken up, and Julia had protested that he shouldn't come out to eat in the kitchen. He just stared her down and told her to leave the room, he was getting up and getting dressed. Jack had bitten back a grin at that, as Julia brushed by him, a thunderous look on her face.

Sliding down onto a chair, Blackie rested his arms on the table, his side burning from the exertion of getting dressed and then walking the few feet to the kitchen. Lord, I can't protect myself or Julia, not just yet. How do I do this?

Jack's hand rested for a moment on his shoulder and Blackie nodded. He looked up at Julia, seeing the concern in her face.

"We'll need to get back to town, Jack. I need to talk to the others." Blackie winced as he looked up and moved slightly.

"We will, Blackie, but not today. Today, I'm heading in. You two are staying here."

"Jack, it's only a few days now to Christmas and my family will be here. I need to see them." Blackie protested.

"Blackie, please. Let Jack go today. Maybe tomorrow he'll let us go. I know Hal and his brother have been arrested, that Mom has disappeared, but he still has men out there that will keep after us. Next time, we might not be so lucky. They almost killed you this time."

Blackie nodded. "I know. I want justice, not revenge I need to be there to see it done."

Jack looked between the young couple, wondering which one of them would prevail, and saw the moment Blackie decided it wasn't worth the fight. Blackie reached for Julia, drawing her close to him and arm around her waist. She wrapped her arms around him and laid her head down. Jack could see her lips moving and knew she was praying.

Blackie finally reached around, pulling Julia down onto his lap, wrapping his arms around her. How do I keep her safe, Lord, when I'm so sore?

Jack paused in drawing on his jacket, watching Blackie. "How be we head into town tomorrow, you two? Your Dad should have everything set up enough to keep you safe."

Blackie snorted, drawing a frown from Julia. "Likely. I'm sure he's working on it. But I don't think all the precautions we're taking will work. They'll find us, somehow, I know."

Jack nodded before he walked away, knowing that Blackie was likely right and that scared him. He didn't want someone close to his niece hurt again, and that was sure to happen.

Julia paced the house later that afternoon. She was bored and didn't know what to do. If they were leaving tomorrow, she would need to make sure the house was tidy and clean. She sighed, shooting a look at Blackie where he sat, engrossed in a book he had found on the shelf. She wouldn't disturb him, she knew. Finding the cleaning supplies, she worked away, ending up in the bedroom she had been using. Jack had mentioned that he wanted to redo it at some point and asked for her opinion. She didn't realize that he had bought the house for her and had intended to give it to her when she turned thirty, a couple of years from then. But that had changed when he saw how she and Blackie cared for one another.

She moved to the window, finding a crack to peer through, as she heard a vehicle. She froze, terror racing through her, as she saw the men who climbed out. She ran for Blackie, pulling him from his chair and with her towards the spare room.

"Julia? Is that Jack out there?" Blackie was bewildered, his book still in his hand.

"No, it's not. Stay here. I'm going after our jackets and boots." She was gone and back in a flash. "Here. Get yours on. Jack told me of a way out of the house and I think we'll have to take it. I don't think they'll know we were here. Jack's made sure of that." She grabbed the book from his hand and placed it on a table, then shoved her feet into her boots and her arms into her coat before heading for the closet and kneeling. "He said there's a trap door here somewhere. It leads downstairs. There are flashlights down there. We can lock it from underneath."

Her scrabbling fingers finally found the latch and she pulled, the door rising easily. She looked up at Blackie. "I need you to go down first. Please, Blackie! Don't be a gentleman at this point."

He nodded, his feet finding the ladder and he scrambled down it, his eyes seeing a flashlight before Julia's movement blocked the light. Partway down, she reached and pulled the door closed, shoving the latch home and then dropping the few feet to stand beside him. They listened to the sound of the door crashing in, the heavy hurried footsteps above them, and the angry shouts and accusations and curses. The sounds finally ceased.

Julia leant back against the ladder, her eyes adjusting slowly to the darkness. Blackie moved to stand beside her, his hand on her arm.

"When do you think it will be safe to go back up?" His voice was low.

"I don't know. Jack didn't say when he would be back. I hate putting him in danger."

"He's done it willingly and I would like to know why." Blackie's hand kept her from moving away.

Julia finally sighed, her chin dropping for a moment. "He's my uncle and I never knew it. My Dad's brother. He's trying to prove Hal and Mom had Dad killed. He said he had proof and was going to talk to Simon."

They heard hurried footsteps overhead and then a low voice calling for Julia and Blackie. They waited, not knowing if it was Jack or not. Finally, the voice raised to a normal level.

"That didn't work. I guess they're not here after all."

"And who said they were? We don't have time to follow false leads." The voice was hard and coarse and Blackie felt Julia tensing under him.

He leaned over close enough to whisper in her ear. "Hal?"

She nodded. "He was supposed to be back in jail." Her voice was equally low. "How'd he get out?"

They waited, Julia making sure that Blackie was not standing, but sitting as much as he could given the small space. They listened, finally hearing new footsteps and quiet voices.

Julia jumped as a tap came to the floor above them and the door was tried.

"Julia, girl. Open up. It's me. I've got Simon with me."

Julia stared at the door for a moment before she felt Blackie's hand on her.

"Go on, Jewel. It's Jack."

She finally nodded, heading up the ladder and sliding the door bolt back, letting Jack lift it up and then reach to help first her and then Blackie from the space. Jack hugged Julia, then stood, hands on her arms and studied her.

"You're okay? They didn't find you, I gather."

She shook her head. "I heard them coming and pulled Blackie down there."

She turned to study the hole, watching as Jack closed it up again. "I wouldn't have known it was there if you hadn't told me."

"That's the whole purpose of it. It was here when I bought the place. I have no idea what the original purpose was for it."

Simon had been speaking quietly with Blackie and now turned to Julia. "Blackie says it was Hal?"

Julia nodded. "It was. I recognized his voice. I think it was his cousin with him." She shivered. "If I hadn't heard them, they'd have taken us, and you would never had found us."

"We know, Julia girl. Now, let's get you back to town. That's what we came for. Simon's made arrangements for a place in town for you."

Julia nodded, her eyes going to Blackie, who was watching her closely. His face was white and she could tell he was in pain. "Let's get going then. Blackie needs to be laying down somewhere."

Simon turned at that and saw what Julia saw, catching his friend as his legs gave way.

"Sorry, guys. I think I did too much." Blackie shook his head.

"That's okay, friend. We need to talk too. I have information that your Dad's dug up that we need to go over."

Blackie nodded, heading for the door. "Then let's go do just that."

Julia watched later as Simon stood, his eyes on Blackie as he slept before he left the room, pulling the door closed behind him.

"Did I hurt him more, Simon, taking him down that ladder?"

Simon shook his head. "No, Doc said you didn't. In fact you probably saved both your lives. Now, we need to talk, Julia. They've proven they will not stop until they find you. We're still trying to determine how they knew you were there. Jack was careful coming and going."

"I know. I think you'll find a lot of homes broken into around the area, with nothing gone. They've been searching the area looking for us and that would have been a logical step."

Simon agreed, before pointing towards Timothy's office. "Let's head there. Jack is waiting for us."

Samuel turned from the window and was at her side before she barely made it into the room, wrapping her into a hug that tightened with feeling. He finally stepped back, blinking his eyes, unable to speak before he led her to the couch and made her sit. He sat beside her, his eyes on Jack, a puzzled look on his face.

Jack turned to Simon. "Any word on Hal or his cousin?"

"We've found the cousin, just waiting on a warrant to arrest him. Hal has disappeared again." Simon was frustrated. "Hal shouldn't have gotten out. Some clerical error they're trying to remedy. He's to go back into custody, if and when we find him."

Samuel turned as he heard a sound from the doorway and then rose, walking towards one of his men, speaking with him for a few minutes before he returned, handing Simon the paperwork he had been given.

"Take a look at that, Simon, and see what you think."

Simon reached for it, his eyes scanning it quickly. "This is great. I'll have one of our detectives verify it, of course, and then we can start making arrests. It should be over soon, Julia."

She stood, pacing, her arms wrapped around herself. "Not soon enough, Simon. Not soon enough." She turned, a hard look on her face. "I want to find him. I want it to all come out what he's done over the years to me and to Jonathan. I want you to say he's a suspect in Dad's death."

Simon nodded. "We can do that. But we have to be careful. He'll come after you. He's mad and he really doesn't care."

She sighed. "I know. I'm trusting God to protect me. We're standing on the edge of bringing him down and returning what should belong to the founding families' descendants. I don't care about that for me, but you four fellows and Finn deserve it."

Simon closed his eyes. She was really going to do that, wasn't she, Lord? "Julia, promise me you won't make a move without talking to me." He finally got her to agree, but knew if she had the chance, she'd go out on her own.

Chapter 16

$\mathcal{J}$ulia watched as Simon headed out, knowing he wasn't happy with her, but also knowing that she wouldn't put lives at risk. He didn't know though that's what she planned to do, put her own life out there and draw Hal out, once and for all.

She moved away from the other men, not seeing them watching her, Jack following to the hall to see where she was heading. She slipped into the room she had been using and searched for her backpack. It was time she moved on and did what she had to do. She didn't realize that in doing so, she would hurt Blackie in a way that she never dreamed of. She quickly packed what she wanted and then slipped out the window, shoving the screen back into place and heading around the house, watching for anyone who was around. Her footsteps led her away from the house and to the downtown, to a building she knew well. She had hidden there many times. She drew a deep breath. Now would come the hard part. Staying out of sight until she could determine where Hal was and draw him out. She needed to do this. Lord, forgive me. Don't let me hurt Blackie too much. He's just not in shape to fight for me and he will. I don't want him to die.

Tears fell as she moved into the darkness of the building, her hand finding the familiar wall and knowing she was almost to the hidden room she had there.

Blackie stirred later, his eyes opening as he stared around before he sat up, scrubbing at his face. He needed to clean up but first he needed to see Julia. He searched the house for her, finally standing at her closed bedroom door, Jack behind him. He tapped. When there was no answer, he reached for the knob, dread filling him.

She was gone, he thought, as he turned a slow circle in the room, his eyes finally resting on Jack, who nodded.

"She slipped away on us, didn't she, boy? Well, I have ways of finding her. She's in hiding somewhere, trying to protect you. That's what she does."

Blackie sighed. "I know. I just wish she hadn't gone. I shouldn't have slept."

"Wouldn't have made any difference, son. She'd have gone anyway." Jack sat on the edge of the bed, pointing Blackie to the easy chair. "You need to understand. When someone is abused, they will shut down. They will try to protect those they love as well by drawing the abuse and attention away from them. That's what she's doing with you."

Blackie nodded, his eyes thoughtful. "I thought we had worked past that. I guess not." He waited but Jack didn't respond. "Now what? I can't just sit here."

"You can and you must, at least until tomorrow. You're still not strong enough to be out there looking for her."

Blackie grew determined. "I will if I have to. If you don't bring me back word tomorrow you've found her, I'll go searching myself. I need her here with me."

"I know you do, son, and we'll find her."

Blackie's face grew bleak. "I know what you're saying but it doesn't bring a lot of comfort." Blackie rose, his balance off for a moment before he headed towards his bedroom. He stood for a moment, eyes on the bed, knowing he should be laying down but not willing to. His father was in the study and he should go talk with him but was reluctant to. He knew his mom and sisters were in town, but he didn't want to see them. They would smother him. He reached for his shoes and then his winter outwear, bundling up and heading for the door, not seeing Jacob watching him.

"Blackie just went out, Simon."

"He did? And just where does he think he's going?" Simon moved towards the door, shrugging into his coat and pulling on his gloves. "Come on. We need to find him."

The two men stood, searching the area, but not seeing Blackie. Blackie had heard the door open and close and slipped behind a tree just down the street. He didn't want them to find him and bring him back there. He was determined to find Julia and find her that night.

Blackie watched as Simon's vehicle headed for the downtown area before he approached the sidewalk once more. He still couldn't believe that his father owned property in this little town. He had grown to love it in the short time he had been there and had no plans to return to his hometown. He knew his mother would have something to say about that.

He approached an abandoned building searching the ground for any footprints and seeing none. He sighed. He moved on, searching over and over again, growing more and more weary. He finally fell to his knees, his arms wrapped around his abdomen, pain staring to course through him. This wasn't such a good idea after all, he thought.

He didn't hear the footsteps approaching him from behind, but felt the hands on his arms, yanking him to his feet and dragging him towards the building he had collapsed in front of. He was shoved inside, falling to his hands and knees, not hearing the coarse loud voice thundering questions at him. He was yanked back to his feet and shoved forward, only a hand on his arm keeping him upright. He drew a deep breath, knowing he had blown it in his determination to find his loved one. He fell facedown on the floor, as the men taunted him and then walked away, leaving him in a crumpled heap, unconscious.

Hours later, a scurrying sound came as quick movements approached him. He was turned over, his pulse felt for, and then he was picked up, the two men carrying him from the building towards a waiting car. He was placed gently inside and then driven to another building. The first man shook his head at the other one's question before they gently lifted Blackie and once more carried him into a building, this time one filled with light and warmth. He was carefully placed on a cot, a blanket pulled over him and the younger man of the two running for the physician that was on site that night.

Julia raised her head from where she lay on a cot near the doorway, hearing the whispers and then rising to follow the men. She stopped in the doorway and as one of them moved caught sight of Blackie. Ignoring their voices as she moved closer, she dropped to her knees, her hand reaching for him.

"Oh, Blackie! Why did you come here? Why aren't you still at home?"

A hand touched her shoulder and the physician spoke to her. "Do you know him?"

She nodded, tears on her cheeks. "I do. He was hurt trying to protect me and I thought if I walked away he would be safe."

"He must love you a lot to have come looking for you. He wasn't hurt again, just collapsed from what Fred here says. They were searching abandoned buildings and found him."

She looked up, pleading on his face. "Is he really okay? He was stabbed and then ran a fever."

"He's fine, child. You can stay with him here in the infirmary. We'll not make you leave." He peered at her again. "You're Julia, aren't you?"

She froze in fear, not sure if she should confirm it or deny it.

"It's okay, child. Old Jack asked me to look out for you. He described you well."

Her eyes slid closed in relief. "Please don't tell anyone I'm here. My stepfather has tried to kill both me and my friend here."

"We'll tell no one. We'll keep you here tonight and then get you somewhere safe tomorrow. I have some place that I think will work. Are the police looking for your stepfather?"

"They are and for his friends." She drew a troubled breath. "No one is safe though. He'll find us and hurt anyone who gets in his way."

"He'll not get in here. We have guards at the doors who will prevent that. You can trust us. Here. Up on your feet. You can use this cot tonight for your rest. I'll be in and out to check on your friend."

He stood just outside the doorway, his eyes on them as he spoke quietly to Fred, who nodded and headed out. He knew Fred would find the man they needed. He turned once more to watch Julia and saw the resemblance to a photo from years ago, one of the founding family's ladies. Then he turned to Blackie and saw something similar to another founding family. Well, he thought, what do we have here?

Jack looked up from where he had slouched in a dark alleyway, hearing cautious steps approaching. Fred stood there, his eyes wandering around the area.

"We have them, Jack. Both of them. Doc'll move them tomorrow before dawn."

Jack nodded. "Good. I was hoping they had found their way there."

"The girl did. Joey and I found the young man. It looks as if he had just been dumped in one of the buildings. If we hadn't seen the footprints, we couldn't have found him."

"God was in this, Fred. Thank you." Fred nodded and walked alway, leaving Jack to head the other way.

Jack drew a deep breath, knowing they were safe, but also knowing he couldn't tell anyone, not even Simon. It was almost Christmas and he needed to get this over with so those two young people would be safe. He had a plan, a plan that might mean his death, but if it saved sweet Julia, he would offer his own life for her.

Julia stirred in the early morning as she felt a hand on her arm. Doc stood there, watching as Fred and Joey carefully helped Blackie to his feet.

"Come, child. We're moving you two. We need to. I have somewhere to put you for the day. Old Jack has been in touch. He knows you're safe He said for you to do what we asked, that he had a plan."

She shook her head. "We can't be together. It's too dangerous."

Doc looked at her. "No, it's dangerous if you split up. If you're together, I can get both of you to safety."

She finally rose, her eyes only on Blackie. He turned as he heard her footsteps and then reached for her, pulling her to him.

"You shouldn't have run, Jewel."

"And you shouldn't have come after me, Blackie."

They were ushered forth building and towards a vehicle. Sudden revving of a motor in the early morning quiet startled all of them and caused them to spin. Doc shoved at the two, yelling at the men to get them out of there, but he was too late. The vehicle was upon them and the men inside flooded out, their hands reaching for Julia and Blackie, shoving Fred, Joey and Doc down and away from them. Bundling the young couple into the vehicle, the driver yelled for the other men to come. The doors were slammed and the vehicle raced away, careening through the streets towards the edge of town.

Doc hurriedly picked himself up, reaching for his phone and calling in the abduction. Frustration grew in all three men as they realized they had been watched, likely all night, for just such an opportunity.

Jack stood watching the men before his eyes lifted towards the distance. This was what he had feared would happen. Now, he had to find them and he had a good idea just where. He turned, surprised to see Simon standing beside him, his breath coming in quick gasps.

"Just missed him. I got word he was here." Simon was getting angry. "Do you know where they are?"

Jack nodded. "I have a good idea. Come with me, Simon. We'll find your friends."

"Let me call in Jacob and Josh first. They'll want in on this."

"And Samuel."

Simon shook his head. "No, not until we find them."

Chapter 17

*S*hoved down into a chair at a table, Julia stared at the papers spread before her and knew Hal was just going to try and make her sign away what she had. She wouldn't and couldn't do it.

Blackie stood against a wall, directly in her line of sight if she raised her eyes. He kept his eyes focused on her, not on the men holding his arms. He was in pain, but not as much as he had been. Whatever the physician had given him, he thought, had finally worked. Or maybe he was just getting better. Or maybe it was the adrenalin coursing through him.

They waited, for how long they never really knew. Julia cringed as she heard heavy, familiar footsteps heading her way. She refused to look up, refused to acknowledge Hal's presence.

Hal stood, anger emanating from him. He hated it when she refused to look at him.

A bully through and through, he wanted acknowledgement of his power and she refused to give it. She always had. This time, he decided, she would or she would die.

He approached her, leaning his hands on the table across from her, waiting for her to cringe back and try to hide from him as was her usual demeanour with him. This time, it didn't happen. She sat, quiet, composed, her eyes on the paperwork, refusing to let him know she knew he was there.

Julia's heart was pounding with fear as she saw Hal's hands come into her vision. She knew only too well how hard they could hit and she just knew they would hit her today, more than likely kill her in Blackie's presence. Lord, why? Why couldn't Blackie have just stayed away? I don't want him to see what I'll go through. Yes, Lord, I know he's seen a lot worse, but this is different. I really thought You had brought him into my life.

Hal's coarse voice broke the silence. "Sign, Julia, and I'll let you go." He waited, but she sat, not responding to his words.

"Not saying anything? That's not like you."
He knew she never said a word in all the
beatings she had taken, knew she never
would, but he still taunted her.

He walked around the table, a hand
roughly raising her chin. She still refused to
look at him.

"Sign the papers, Julia, and I'll let you
and your friend here go." When she refused
to speak, his hand moved quickly, leaving
redness on her face and blood on her lip. He
heard movement from behind him and
laughed, knowing Blackie was trying to get
away.

"Sign, Julia. The next blow goes to
your friend."

Julia's eyes raised to Blackie, seeing
his love for her in his, and signalling hers
back. The strength of character she had
always found in him shone through and she
drew from that, knowing that if this was the
end for them, he loved her in a way no one
had ever.

She shook her head. "That's not
happening , Hal. I can't sign those. It's not

mine to give away.   If you knew the town history, you'd know that."

He flicked his fingers in the air.   "Just an old piece of paper.   Not legal any more."   He slammed a hand on the table, expecting her to jump.   When she didn't, he stepped back to assess her.   What had changed, he wondered?   She is refusing to behave like she always had.   He turned his eyes towards Blackie and found steady eyes on him.

He pointed at Blackie.   "You're the reason she won't sign."

Blackie shook his head, sorrow for he man in his eyes.   "No, actually, I'm not.   I have no say in what she does or doesn't do.   She's free to make her own decisions, likely for the first time in her life."   That comment earned Blackie his own blow across the face.

He straightened, his eyes on Julia, finding her steady in her determination not to cave

No matter the threats, the blows, the beatings they took, both stood firm in their determination not to give in to a bully.   They drew strength from one another.

Hal was angry, angrier than he had ever been, and that anger drove him to make a mistake. He walked away from the two for a moment, rage coursing through him, blinding him, absorbing everything in him. He had murder plotted in his heart, murder of those two. It would mean he would never get what he wanted, but he just couldn't abide someone standing up to him and winning.

He didn't hear the footsteps approaching quietly as he turned and raged back towards the two, a hand reaching for his revolver and pulling it out. Blackie looked up with blurring eyes, seeing that and drawing strength to wrest his arms from the two men holding him and throwing himself at Hal. They struggled, each fighting for control on the revolver, the weapon gradually being forced between them. Julia watched in horror, praying, begging for God to spare Blackie. A sudden jolt of sound and the men froze even as footsteps were heard running towards them.

Julia screamed as she saw Blackie falling. She threw herself towards him, drawing him away from Hal, searching for blood and finding none. He raised himself to a sitting position, pulling her to him and just held her as tight as he could, his head down on her hair as she clung to hm, sobbing. His eyes focused on Hal even as he heard voices and confusion around him.

A gentle hand on his shoulder finally raised his head. Samuel crouched beside him, tears on his face as he realized his son was finally safe.

"Dad?"

"I'm here, son." Samuel's arms reached to hug the couple, knowing that Blackie would not let go of his lady. "You're safe, son. Both of you. Simon says they've found everyone involved. The police just have to sort everything out, but he thinks it will be after Christmas now when that happens." He looked up at the approaching paramedics. "Let's get you looked at, okay?"

Blackie finally nodded, his hand going to Julia's cheek, frowning as she winced. "Jewel, we'll get checked out and then head home. We're not going to the hospital. That I can guarantee you." He looked at his father. "Mom and the girls are here?"

"They are, Levi. They are so worried, I'm not sure you'll want to come back to the B&B." He gave a low laugh at Blackie's frown and then quick grin.

Two hours later, Julia turned from where she had been brushing her hair. She had showered and taken the clean clothes Finn had handed her, brand new ones she noted, with a quiet word of thanks. It was finally over, she thought. I am finally free of the monster.

She headed for the kitchen, suddenly hungry, knowing Mary would have food ready for them. She stopped as she saw Blackie standing in the study, staring out the window, hands shoved into his pockets.

She paused in the doorway, not sure if she should approach him or not. He turned, his hand reaching for hers.

Cradling her close to him, Blackie thanked the Lord she was here, was safe, and finally could move on with her life. Whether that included him or not remained to be seen.

"Blackie? Thank you for all you did. I don't think I could have made it through without you."

He said nothing, knowing that words were not needed. She tilted her head, reading his face correctly.

She finally spoke. "It's almost Christmas, Blackie. I will enjoy it this year for the first time since before Dad died. I want to know what happened, but that doesn't change anything about you. You are the one I want to spend Christmas with."

Blackie studied her face, knowing she was speaking the truth. "You're sure? I don't want us to commit and then have you decide you need to walk away. I'll give you the time you need now."

She shook her head. "I know now, Blackie. God has shown me without a doubt. I never dreamed that I would ever be free, that I would meet someone like you."

Blackie finally nodded and reached into a pocket, pulling out a ring with a ruby stone in it. "This was my grandmother, on my Mom's side. Grandfather bought it for Grandmother, always saying she was more precious than rubies. That's how I feel about you."

Tears sparkled as she held out her hand. "I love that, Blackie. That's how you make it feel."

He swept her close, his blond head lowering as he sought her lips. He didn't see his mother stop in the doorway and then retreat, her own tears close as she sought out Samuel, who just gave her a look and swept her close to his own heart. All was right in their world for once, and just in time for the Christmas they wanted to have.

Christmas Day passed, full of laughter, fun and tears. Blackie and Julia had taken a lot of teasing, as had Jacob and Finn, leaving Josh and Simon wistful for ladies of their own.

Simon had worked hard up to Christmas Day and then was back at it a couple of days later. It would take weeks of investigations and serving warrants to determine exactly what all Hal had been involved in, but he was determined to do just that.

❄ ❄ ❄ ❄ ❄ ❄

Simon was on a hunt. It was near the end of January and he knew Blackie and Julia were at his place, making their final plans before their wedding to take place three days from then. He needed to see them. He had, he thought, the final investigation done and he wanted to inform them of the results.

He paused at the door, a frown appearing as he heard a raised female voice, raised in anger and accusation. That's not Julia, he thought. He tried the doorknob, finding it turning under his hand and entered, his feet as silent as he could make them, slipping from his jacket and throwing it on a chair. He moved forward, stopping before he would be seen. He listened and realized that here was the piece he thought was missing and hadn't been able to discover. Julia's mother. She was part of this and they had not been able to prove it. Now they could, by her own words.

Simon finally stepped into view, catching Blackie's eyes as he stood, his arm around Julia as she faced her mother. Julia was not backing down at all from her, taking the accusations and guilt thrown at her and letting it roll off her.

Simon finally reached for the woman's arm and pulled it behind her, cuffs slapped on her wrists, placing her under arrest. He led her from the room, his phone out to make the call he had dreaded but knowing it was necessary. A few words with the responding officers and he approached Blackie and Julia again.

"Julia? Are you okay?" He was concerned. This was her mother, after all.

She nodded, a light on her face he had not seen before. "Thank you, Simon. I am. I finally am. She has no control over me any more. Thank you, Lord, that happened before we married, Blackie." She turned in his arms, her own arms going around him. "That would have cast a huge shadow on us."

"It would have, love, but we'd have worked through it. I know you're still going for counselling with the pastor and will for months to come. But you're finally healing." Blackie's arm tightened on her and he looked at Simon, a frown on his face. "Simon? How did you come to be here?"

Simon laughed, even as he shook his head. "That's a story in itself. I never expected to find her here, but it does wrap up any loose ends. I just wanted to let you two know that Hal's brother and cousin have talked, taking a plea deal, as have some of the other men. They've been sentenced and will spend time in jail.

"Hal has refused to confess, refused actually to talk with us. He asked for a lawyer as soon as we arrested him and that meant he said nothing. But we have enough evidence to put him away for the rest of his life. The charges include extortion, assault, and murder. We haven't even got to you yet, Julia, and what he will face for that." He held up a hand at her protest. "I know you don't want to, but you need to, as part of your healing process." He paused, sorrow flickering across his face.

"We did find evidence that, as you suspected, he had your father killed. Old Jack helped out that way. He said he had a vested interest in that, but that you would have to be the one to explain."

"I'm glad that is finally settled. Now that I know, I can accept it and move on." She turned in Blackie's arms, her head resting against his strong chest, feeling the love he had for her in how he held her. "Old Jack." A smile spread across her face. "Yes, Old Jack, as he wants to be called. I think it's time the town recognized him for who he is. He's been here, back in his home town, giving an impression that he's homeless, but he's not. I'm sure you found that out, Simon." She paused, her face tilting as she looked up at Blackie, getting his nod, before looking back at Simon.

Her voice was low and full of love as she continued. "You see, Simon, he's not homeless. He is a vet, but he's not homeless. And yes, he does have a vested interest in finding out who killed Dad. He's my Uncle Ben, my father's only brother."

Simon's movements stilled. Whatever he had expected to hear, this was not it. "Your uncle?"

"My uncle. Josh figured it out, Uncle Ben said, weeks ago."

"And he never said a word. It was hinted at, but I never picked that up. Or if I did, I forget. Now, I'm not sure which is is." Simon was shaking his head.

"Uncle Ben asked him not to, just to keep it quiet until this was resolved. Now, Jonathan can come home too." Her face lit up at the thought. "I can't wait for that to happen. It will be so good to have him around again."

"I'm sure it will. Listen, I'm out of here. I'll be in touch, Julia, about the charges against your mother." He waved as he walked away.

Blackie stood, his love in his arms, his chin on her head. "Did you ever decide who's walking you downtime aisle on Saturday?"

She shrugged. "Last I heard, I had both Uncle Ben and Jonathan doing the honours. It will be interesting to see how we manage that."

He turned her to face him, his eyes searching her. "And you're okay with all this?"

She nodded. "I am. I love you so much."

$\mathcal{S}$ix months later, Blackie looked up from his work as he heard laughter from the kitchen and smiled. Rachel and Rebecca had dropped in and insisted that Julia needed to go shopping with them. Blackie's family had relocated to town, and he was glad. They fit so well into the town and were loved by many. Miriam had become part of the work Blackie had stared for the youth and become a grandmother figure to many. His father continued to run his business from there and was also part of the church family, reaching out to help anyone who needed it.

Julia appeared in the doorway, her hand reaching for him. "Come on, sweetheart. We need you out here. We're trying to get a lunch ready for the family and need your help."

He gave an exaggerated sigh and rose, smiling as she grinned at him, stopping to gather her close and steal kisses from her until she pushed at him.

"Come on. The girls really do need our help."

He laughed, even as he kissed her again. "Really? I like where I am right now."

She blushed, something he often caused just by teasing her. "So do I, but come on. I really do need you to come to the kitchen."

He took her hand and followed as she pulled him forward, stopping in the doorway as he saw the decorated room and his family and friends standing there. He was puzzled, not sure what the occasion was.

"Julia?" He turned, finding her in tears. "What's going on?"

Samuel moved forward, his arm going around his much loved daughter-in-law. "This was Julia's idea, Levi. She finally got word that her book has been accepted by a small publisher, who wants to use it to forward the cause for help for abuse victims. We're so proud of her, Levi."

Blackie's eyes sought his wife's, seeing the uncertainty there. "Your book? I didn't realize you had finished it."

"I did, about a month ago. I didn't tell you because I didn't think it would be accepted anywhere. The publisher has been great. We're setting up a trust fund to help with counselling for those who need it. I hope we can work it through the centre as well."

He hugged her tight, feeling her tears soak his shirt. "I think this is just wonderful. Just like you, love." Tears blocked his sight until he blinked. "And what title did you come up with?"

She started laughing, bringing laughter from those around him. "Mistletoe Medicine. Subtitle. Healing from Abuse."

"I like that, Julia. It's so you."

They moved away, mingling with the group, laughter and tears part of their afternoon, all part of a healing process started when Julia had been freed so many months ago from the cycle of abuser and victim.

Dear Reader:

Thank you for picking up the story of Blackie and Julia. It is not the story I imagined for him. She was not the lady I pictured for him, but she was what he needed. An abuse victim and a hero, a medic who had seen horrible things, but survived and who could understand her trauma.

Abuse, unfortunately, is prevalent in society today, a lot of it hidden. My admiration goes to the women, children, and yes, men, who make the decision that they will no longer be a victim and seek help.

But, and there is always a but, God sees what is happening and is there, even in the darkest days. He sees what man does not. It is my prayer that people will turn to Him, especially in these dark days.

Blackie and Julia - what a couple! Thank you for sharing their story. And sigh, I can see Jonathan and Old Jack wanting their stories told. Old Jack, or Uncle Ben, was not to be such a strong character in the book, but these characters have a way of making their way into a book and building their stories. Demanding characters, they can be, and throwing in plot challenges and side roads is all part of it.

God bless each one of you. May you seek His presence daily.

Ronna

9 781989 000588